·*A*
Harlequin
Romance

OTHER
Harlequin Romances
by IRIS DANBURY

Many of these titles are available at your local bookseller,
or through the Harlequin Reader Service.

For a free catalogue listing all available Harlequin Romances,
send your name and address to:

HARLEQUIN READER SERVICE,
M.P.O. Box 707, Niagara Falls, N.Y. 14302
Canadian address: Stratford, Ontario, Canada.

or use coupon at back of book.

THE AMETHYST MEADOWS

by

IRIS DANBURY

HARLEQUIN BOOKS   TORONTO
WINNIPEG

Original hard cover editon published in 1974
by Mills & Boon Limited.

© Iris Danbury 1974

SBN 373-01837-1

Harlequin edition published December, 1974

Printed in Canada

CHAPTER ONE

IN her whole life Averil had never experienced such inordinate disappointment. She had come to Spain with such high hopes, confident that she would find the country as glowing and exciting as the travel posters portrayed—sunshine, colour, a land of exotic flowers, the whirling excitement of flamenco and all the rest of the paradise that spelt the magic of Spain.

The reality was totally different.

A letter from a lawyer in Seville had started this adventure. Three weeks ago Averil called on her great-aunt Freda and found her very excited.

'Look, Averil dear. This has just come. From Seville.' She thrust the letter at Averil. 'Dear Francisco has left me a house and some property in Spain. After all these years! So he never forgot me.'

Averil had heard from her own father of his Aunt Freda's romance so long ago, when she had refused to marry the handsome Francisco and go to Spain with him, but stayed at home to care for her mother.

'What a lovely surprise!' was Averil's comment.

'The lawyer says there are certain complications and if I could go to Seville to sign a few papers——' The older woman broke off with a wistful smile. 'But that's out of the question, of course.'

Averil nodded. It was not old age, for Freda was only in her early sixties, but the fact that she was crippled with arthritis and could walk only with difficulty.

'So how would you like to go in my place?'

The sudden question disconcerted Averil. 'But I wouldn't know how to cope with business affairs like this.'

'Dear Averil, you have the most practical head on your shoulders. Your father can easily spare you from your office work and you could spend a marvellous summer in Spain— and do me a favour at the same time. I'll pay all your expenses, of course.'

'Let me think it over,' suggested Averil.

The proposal had taken surprisingly little time to put into practice. Averil worked in her father's small stationery and printing business in a quiet Somerset town, and although he grumbled at first, he finally agreed to release her for two or three months.

Averil's mother was more dubious. 'I'm not sure that I like the idea of your roaming around Spain alone.'

'Don't be silly, Mummy,' put in Dinah, Averil's younger sister. 'She'll be swept off her feet by any amount of handsome Spaniards and have the most exciting time of her life. I wish I were going.'

Since Dinah was a bare fourteen, the plan was out of the question, but now Averil regretted that some other member of her family could not have come to this lesser-known part of Spain.

She had imagined that the estate her great-aunt had inherited was perhaps only a few miles from Seville, but she discovered that it was much nearer the south-west coast and on the edge of the swamplands called Las Marismas. There had been no one to meet her at Seville and when she showed taxi-drivers the address, they shook their heads and refused. Eventually she was able to hire a car which took her towards Cadiz and then branched off along a muddy track between flat swampy fields dotted with pools.

Evidently she had not been expected at the villa. 'But I am Señorita Sanderson,' she told the man who opened the door. 'I wrote to you.'

He gave no sign of welcome. Then she showed him her passport and one of the letters from the lawyer in Seville. Reluctantly, it seemed, he summoned a woman who prepared a bedroom while Averil ate a hastily assembled meal.

She had now been here two days and the rain had scarcely ceased. As she stared out from her small balcony over the untidy garden and beyond, the vine terraces and then the melon fields, she wondered how long she could endure this grey, sodden landscape. The best thing would be to go to Seville, tidy up the legal points with the lawyer in the shortest possible time and leave for home.

She had already inspected the villa and was dismayed to

6

find so much neglect. The wall panelling in the main rooms was broken in many places, ceilings looked as though any slight vibration would bring them down in a shower of dust. Everywhere the paintwork was blistered or worn down to the bare rotting wood. The whole place was a liability rather than an asset and Averil considered it would have been better if Great-aunt Freda had never been told of an inheritance of such dubious value.

There was a suspicious atmosphere about the place that Averil found disquieting. The man Gonzalo who appeared to be in charge and his wife Marta who did the cooking both treated her as an unwelcome stranger.

'I want to go to Seville,' she told Gonzalo when she found him in the courtyard. 'Is there a car here and some-one who can drive?'

He shrugged. 'No car.'

'Then will you please order one for me for ten o'clock.'

'Not possible,' answered Gonzalo stolidly.

'Why not? You can telephone.'

'No telephone.'

'No telephone? But I saw one in the hall.'

'Not working.'

She gave the man a glance of disbelief, but when she picked up the old-fashioned receiver, the line was obviously dead.

Gonzalo had silently followed her into the hall. 'Then send a messenger. I need a car and I want it this morning.'

On previous occasions Gonzalo had affected not to under-stand Averil's tolerable Spanish, but now he gave her a sly smile. 'There are horses, also good donkeys, if the señorita would like to ride.'

Averil glared at him. 'I don't want to ride all the way to Seville,' she said firmly.

'Perhaps I ask Don Rodrigo to find a car for Seville,' suggested Gonzalo.

'Please do so.'

'He lives near. He has several cars.'

Averil went up to her room to sort out some of the papers she wanted to take to the lawyer in Seville. When she came down again and stepped outside the front door, a tall man with a tanned face and dark brown hair was talking in rapid Spanish to Gonzalo.

'Don Rodrigo?' she queried. 'I hope it is not——' she began in Spanish.

'I'm not Don Rodrigo,' the man answered in English.

'No, this is Señor Brunner,' put in Gonzalo hastily, adding, 'the *señorita* is also from England.'

The man called Brunner regarded Averil with interest. 'Oh, indeed? What brings you to this out-of-the-way place?'

'Business matters,' she replied a trifle brusquely. 'If you have the car, shall we go?'

Gonzalo was hurrying across the patio towards the road that ran outside the villa.

'Certainly,' Mr. Brunner appeared faintly amused. 'But I'm not sure that I understand, Miss—er——'

'Sanderson. Averil Sanderson,' she supplied.

'I'm Connall Brunner and I'm working near here at present. If I can give you a lift somewhere——'

'I understood that Gonzalo was arranging for a car to take me to Seville, but he spoke of——'

At that moment Gonzalo came running back.

'Here is Don Rodrigo,' he shouted. 'He has the car.'

Averil smiled at Mr. Brunner. 'Oh, I see I've made a mistake.'

'You'll find the noble Spaniard's car much more comfortable than mine,' he answered as he accompanied her towards the road.

Gonzalo was now all politeness and smiles as he made the introductions. 'Allow me, *señorita*, to present Don Rodrigo de Montilla.'

Averil was confronted by a man slightly taller and darker than Mr. Brunner.

'You would like to go to Seville.' Don Rodrigo spoke in fluent English.

'Yes, if it's convenient.'

'But of course. No trouble.'

As he drove away from the villa, Averil saw Mr. Brunner standing outside, his hand raised in a gesture of farewell.

Don Rodrigo had driven about a mile along the wet,

soggy road when he asked, 'May one know why you have come to this unfrequented part of Spain?'

'My great-aunt Freda has apparently inherited the property, which I believe is called the Villa Serena. The previous owner was someone called Francisco. I don't know his surname.'

'And you have come to claim it?'

She nodded. 'There are apparently legal matters to deal with first.'

For some minutes her companion drove in silence and she turned her head to study him. A lean face with aquiline nose and strongly marked eyebrows; a firm jawline and black, shining hair.

He turned towards her with a half smile. 'You are satisfied with your inspection, *señorita*?'

She reddened slightly. 'I'm sorry. I didn't mean to stare so rudely.'

'Not in the least. I am quite flattered. I have already studied your very pretty face in the mirror. You are unmistakably English-looking.'

'I suppose so.' With her corn-coloured hair cut to shoulder length, dark blue eyes and fair skin, she realised that she was a complete contrast to the colouring of most Spanish girls.

'I must apologise for not calling on you earlier, *señorita*. But I returned from Madrid only last night and I was told this morning that you had come to look at Don Francisco's estate.'

So he had already known why she was here, Averil reflected, but she made no comment.

'Will it be convenient for you to wait in Seville and drive me back?' she asked. 'I don't want to be a nuisance.'

He smiled. 'One so charming could hardly be counted a nuisance. Naturally I shall wait.'

'You are a neighbour of Francisco?'

'I own the estate that adjoins. It is perhaps larger than the Serena property. You must allow me to show it to you while you are staying here.'

'Thank you.' Averil realised that she might need all the help she could get from neighbours of adjoining estates.

9

Don Rodrigo escorted her to the lawyer's office in Seville, but disappointment was the only result, for the lawyer was away in Madrid and would not return for several days.

'Of ourse I should have made a definite appointment,' admitted Averil, 'but I did write before I left England and told him I would be coming as soon as possible after I arrived.'

Don Rodrigo smiled. 'Then you must allow me to make amends for the delay by taking you to lunch.'

He had parked the car in a small *plaza* and now conducted her along a narrow street closed to traffic.

'This is the Calle de los Sierpes,' he explained. 'You see it winds like a serpent, as it is named.'

The street was lined with shops selling fans and pictures, religious ornaments and leather work. Groups of men stood about chatting or sitting at tables outside the clubs and wine-shops, and Don Rodrigo was greeted by a number of his acquaintances as he and Averil strolled through.

'One of the business places of the city,' he explained. 'People don't visit each other's offices so much. They come here at midday and discuss their plans and agreements over a glass of wine.'

Here, at least, thought Averil, was some of the colour and bustle of a lively Spanish town.

'It's quite a contrast to the surroundings of the Serena estate,' she commented.

Don Rodrigo smiled. 'A great deal of Spain is quite different from the usual idealised versions of sunny beaches and exotic dancers.'

'I know, but we get a certain picture in our minds and it's difficult to adjust to a different reality.'

'You do not care for our part of Las Marismas?' he queried, and she heard a slight eagerness in his tone. Perhaps he, too, did not welcome an intruder into the district, particularly one trying to claim an inheritance.

He took her to a restaurant facing the river. Averil rather reluctantly tried *gazpacho*, the chilled soup of tomatoes and spicy peppers recommended by Don Rodrigo.

'You are accustomed to hot soups?'

'Usually, although I've tried Vichyssoise and liked that.'

10

She allowed him to choose the rest of the meal, a fish medley called *zarzuela* followed by small strips of meat in a piquant sauce and finally fresh fruit.

'Tell me how it is that you have a relative who now inherits the Serena estate,' he directed over the coffee.

Averil smiled. 'I think it's a long story, of which I know only a small part. My great-aunt Freda—my father's aunt, you understand—was in love with Francisco, but would not leave her mother and go to live in Spain. Did Francisco every marry?'

'As far as I know, he did not.'

'So there are no children to complicate matters.'

'No children in the direct line, but there are several nephews, nieces, cousins and so on. You may find that the lawyer already has received claims from some of these people.'

'But in that case how is it that the whole place, the estate, the villa, everywhere, has been so neglected?' she demanded. 'If some of these other relatives wanted to inherit, they might have tried keeping the place in proper repair.'

She spoke heatedly and he gave her a glance of approval.

'This happens everywhere, in every country. People do not want the bother, the responsibility, but when the owner dies, they want their share of what is left.'

Averil reflected that this was undoubtedly true. 'Then the sooner I see the lawyer, the better. I shall know then how I stand—or rather what will eventually come to my great-aunt.'

'I will make an appointment for you,' Don Rodrigo promised. 'Then I can bring you again to Seville on that day.'

'But are you sure you don't mind? I've no wish to become a——'

'A nuisance? You must not take such a modest view of yourself, *señorita*, or with lawyers and possible hangers-on you will never get anywhere.'

As he spoke she met his glance again. His dark eyes danced with flattering admiration. She tried to sustain her own uncompromising stare, but was forced to lower her lids. This was altogether much too soon to be enslaved by a touch of Latin blandishment.

During the afternoon Don Rodrigo hired a horse-drawn carriage and took Averil on a sightseeing tour.

'This is not the way to see our beautiful city,' he pointed out. 'Only a preliminary tour. One must walk on foot to notice the buildings and the gardens and parks, but you will be able to come many times and explore for yourself.'

She enjoyed this leisurely way of seeing the Gold Tower, a glimpse of the cathedral, the famous Santa Cruz quarter and promised herself that she would spend as much time as she could finding her way about this lovely city.

'I suppose it might be an idea if I were to transfer to Seville and stay here in a small hotel or pension. Then I could come out to the Villa Serena whenever it was necessary.'

He frowned. 'Some advantages, some disadvantages. Wait until you have seen the lawyer.'

Once again she heard that slight inflection that alerted her to more careful choice of words. Don Rodrigo appeared to be a friendly neighbour and at the present time an attentive host, but she was not yet sure on so slender an acquaintance whether she could trust him with her confidence.

When at last he dismissed the carriage driver, he took Averil to a park restaurant for coffee and delicious little cakes.

'In a short time it will be quite dark,' he said. 'Then you will see Seville come alive with lights. Fountains, too.'

The *plazas* were brilliantly lit and down by the river reflections glittered on the dark water.

'We could have dinner here in Seville, if you choose, or go back to my villa where I shall be most happy to entertain you.'

Averil considered his suggestion for a moment or two. If she chose dinner here the drive home to the Villa Serena would land her there at a late hour. Yet she did not feel equal to meeting the rest of Don Rodrigo's family on this occasion at the end of a busy day, particularly when she considered that she was not dressed for the event.

'Perhaps we could have a small snack somewhere?' she

suggested as a compromise. 'I'm not very hungry. Then this would perhaps be more convenient for your own meal at your home.'

His dark eyes lit with amusement. 'You are most determined not to give me trouble, aren't you?'

The snack bar was fairly full, but Don Rodrigo found a couple of stools at the end of the counter where a large variety of food was displayed. Averil ate very little, but was glad of the strong coffee. Her companion dealt with a chicken salad, some kind of pastry with fruit and a bottle of wine.

Averil hoped that the wine would not affect his driving and as though he had read her thoughts, he remarked, 'One must be fortified for driving. I do not drive well if I have not eaten properly.'

In the car the lights of Seville were soon well behind and Averil saw little but the darkened landscape or the edge of the road illumined by the headlights.

'You have enjoyed this day?' he asked after some miles.

'Very much indeed.'

'Then you must allow me to take you on many visits, not only to Seville, but to other places, Cadiz, parts of the coast, even perhaps Madrid, for I go there sometimes.'

Averil murmured a controlled 'Thank you,' although inwardly she was eager enough to repeat excursions out and about with Don Rodrigo. Yet she must beware of falling headlong in love with the first handsome Spaniard she met.

Gonzalo eyed her with interest when she entered the villa from the courtyard and Don Rodrigo had driven away.

'You have seen the lawyer?' he inquired.

'No. He was away. I shall go another time.'

It was surely not her fancy that Gonzalo's dark, leathery features held a satisfied smile.

Don Rodrigo had promised to make an appointment for her in Seville with the lawyer during the next few days, so she had leisure to explore the surroundings of the villa.

Gonzalo accompanied her the next morning and pointed out the various sections, the vines, melons, a few olives and a rice field.

'Rice?' she queried. 'I'd no idea that grew in Spain.'

13

'Only where it is wet,' Gonzalo assured her.

'It's certainly a wet part here.' Although the rain had ceased, the sky was still leaden grey and promised a further downpour at any time. Yesterday Seville had been so different. The sun had been shining, enriching the deep russet colours of the Cathedral and the beautiful Giralda tower, sparkling on the fountain jets and lighting the pale green mist of the budding trees.

Here on the Serena estate there seemed nothing that looked prosperous. How could it be when everything was bedraggled by incessant rain?

She turned towards Gonzalo. 'Does it also rain all the summer?' At that moment a young lad came running behind them, shouting for Gonzalo. The boy spoke rapidly in Spanish, but Averil could not quite understand the words and assumed that he was using a local dialect.

Gonzalo touched his hat in a brief casual gesture. 'I must return, *señorita*. It is nothing important. But come with me.'

'No,' she decided. 'I'll walk about a little more on my own.'

Gonzalo hurried off with the boy and Averil surveyed the remaining part of the estate. Actually, she was not sure exactly where the boundaries were fixed, but there were no fences, so she walked across a stretch of firm land that seemed to have been prepared for some other crop or plantation. The vestige of a path lay ahead and she plunged along the rough tussocks, but suddenly she found herself in a pool with the water up to her knees.

Desperately she tried to extricate her feet, but succeeded only in sprawling forward on her knees.

A voice behind her called 'Wait!' but she was in no position to turn and see the owner. Almost immediately strong hands grasped her shoulders and dragged her upright, then pulled her to firmer ground.

'Heavens, you look a mess!' exclaimed her rescuer, whom she saw now was the Englishman, Mr. Brunner. 'You shouldn't try promenading about these parts, or at least not until the marshes have dried out in high summer.'

'I missed my footing,' she said crossly.

14

'Then you should take a horse or even a donkey. They are always careful where they put their dainty feet. You'd be much safer.'

'I shouldn't,' she contradicted. 'I can't ride a horse and I'm not sure I want to sit on a donkey.'

She glared ruefully at her soaked trousers, and suede shoes. Then she looked up and met his glance. 'I suppose I ought to thank you, but I shouldn't have drowned, you know. The water wasn't as deep as that.'

His firm mouth tightened. 'Not here on your estate, perhaps, but take my advice and don't be so venturesome in future or you might end up in a muddy hole. Plenty of animals are lost that way.'

'It seems a dangerous part of the country,' she retorted.

'Only to those who take unnecessary risks,' he snapped.

His harsh tone subdued her for a few moments. She looked at his clothes, strong breeches and boots, a thick jacket and a polo-necked sweater.

'I see that I must dress more appropriately for this kind of country,' she admitted with a half smile. 'I'd no idea when I came that it would be like this.'

'Ah! Come to Sunny Spain, all oranges and girls with flowers in their hair. And does this wet reality disappoint you?'

'Yes,' she answered decisively. 'If I'd known, I think I might have advised my great-aunt Freda not to accept this so-called inheritance. The surroundings are a marshy wilderness, the estate looks miserably neglected and the villa is practically falling down.'

'I see. So you'd have been a quitter without even looking at the land.'

She turned sharply towards him. 'I'm not here on my own behalf.'

'Then tell me about your position,' he invited, as he walked his horse along the track, with Averil beside him.

'Don't you know already from Gonzalo?'

'I probably do, but I'd like to hear the facts from you. Gonzalo sometimes twists a tale if it's to his own advantage.'

Briefly she explained the events that had led to her arri-

15

val here. 'There appears to be some legal business to settle,' she continued. 'As soon as that is finished, I shall of course leave.'

He laughed. 'Legal business in Spain can easily keep you here for a couple of years. Even if everything is then settled in your relative's favour, by that time your rascally foreman, Gonzalo, will have drained the estate of most of its value and you'll be left with a piece of worthless property that won't even pay the legal expenses.'

She stopped walking and stared up at him. 'Do you really mean that or are you saying it just to annoy me?'

He stared back and his hazel eyes held amusement and perhaps something else that Averil could not quite fathom.

'My dear Señorita Sanderson—or am I allowed to call you Averil? If I were in the mood, I could think of any number or ways to annoy you, but just at this moment I'm doing my best to warn you of what's in store.'

'Any suggestions?' she asked crisply.

'Yes. Don't trust Gonzalo. Tell him as little as possible. Also, I think you might be rather careful how much confidence you place in Don Rodrigo de Montilla. I know you went to Seville with him yesterday and I hope you enjoyed yourself.'

'Yes, I did. Don Rodrigo was a charming host. He took me about, showed me some of the sights——'

'But made sure that you wouldn't see the lawyer?'

'How could he know in advance that the man wasn't there?'

Connall Brunner turned his head and smiled at her. 'There is precious little he doesn't know. Remember he's been a neighbour of Don Francisco for a long time. If he doesn't know all the history of the district at first hand, his father and the rest of the family are well acquainted with it all.'

'Aren't you being rather unfair?' she asked.

'You'll have to find that out for yourself, won't you?' he countered.

She was affronted by his brusque manner, yet she did not want to lose the opportunity of discovering everything she could about the Serena estate as well as Don Rodrigo's.

'You said that Gonzalo was a rascally foreman. Does that mean he takes the profits out of the estate for himself?'

'He's probably been doing that for years. Don Francisco was an old man. I met him a few times in the past year and all he seemed to need was food and drink, a bed to sleep in and enough leisure time to spend over his books. He left the running of the estate almost entirely in Gonzalo's hands, and that was probably a mistake.'

'Books, did you say?' she queried. 'What sort of books?'

'The old man had a fine collection of early editions— Spanish, Italian, French, German, probably others. Haven't you looked over the villa yet?'

'Yes, more or less. But I didn't see any room that looked like a library.'

'Then have another look. If Gonzalo has discovered that the books have any value, he'll probably sell them.'

'Which room would they be in?' Averil asked.

'Some in a study on the ground floor—a room in that wing that runs along the side of the patio. I think Don Francisco also had a store in one of the rooms upstairs.'

'Thank you for telling me.' She shot him a grateful smile. 'You seem to know a great deal about this district and the people. Do you live here?'

'More or less, for the time being. I work on the roads. But this is where I leave you. You're in sight of the Villa Serena and that path up there is fairly solid. But don't chance any marshy bits or you'll find yourself in trouble.'

He mounted his hourse with an easy, lithe movement.

'Thank you, Mr. Brunner, for your help.'

'Think nothing of it. I'm quite accustomed to hauling girls out of swamps.' He rode off and for a few moments she stood there gazing after him. Then she walked back to the villa. In her bedroom she stripped off the muddy light blue trousers and soiled white jumper and put on a light-weight woollen dress. The temperature of the house was not very high, she thought, but perhaps it was more the damp atmosphere that gave it a chilly air.

Her first idea was to search for Don Francisco's study and his books, but when she went to the wing that at some time earlier had been built on to the older part of the villa

17

Marta, Gonzalo's wife, came towards her.

'You need something, *señorita*?' the woman asked.

'I'd like to see Don Francisco's——' Averil broke off. 'I don't think I've seen all over the villa,' she amended. 'Perhaps there are some rooms I've missed.' She was trying not to arouse any suspicion on the part of Marta, a middle-aged woman who had undoubtedly been a handsome girl with dark flashing eyes and a crown of black hair.

Now she gave Averil an appraising stare. 'Which rooms, *señorita*?'

'This one, for instance.' Averil tried the door in front of her. It was locked. 'You have the key?'

'One moment and I bring it.' She went towards the part of the villa where the kitchen was situated, but she was absent for a long time and Averil tried several other doors, most of which yielded. Several were only sparsely furnished and in one a carpet was rolled up and tied with rope. There were signs that once this villa had been elegantly and luxuriously furnished, but now the tables and chairs, the writing desks and pictures were shamefully neglected.

Gonzalo himself eventually returned with the key of the locked room. As she had expected, this was Don Francisco's study, but where were the books? Most of the shelves were empty.

'Where are Don Francisco's books?' she demanded of Gonzalo.

He shrugged. 'Someone came—from the lawyer—and took them away.'

'To be valued?'

'How should I know?'

She examined the rosewood writing desk. One of the locks had evidently been forced. She pulled open one drawer after another. All that remained were a few dusty papers.

'All the papers have gone to the lawyer in Seville,' Gonzalo announced quickly, as though anxious to clear himself of an accusation not yet made.

Averil regarded him steadily, but his bold, black eyes did not waver.

'I will keep the key of this room,' she said, 'although

there seems to be little in it worth locking up.'

'As you desire, *señorita*.' There was a hint of ridicule in the exaggerated bow that he gave her as he went out of the room.

Later in the day Don Rodrigo called to inform Averil that he had telephoned the lawyer's office in Seville and made an appointment for the following Tuesday.

'If that day suits you, it will give me great pleasure to drive you into Seville.'

'Thank you, Don Rodrigo.' She accepted without hesitation, for in spite of Connall Brunner's warning, she must make contact with the lawyer.

After she had instructed Marta to serve wine to the visitor, Averil spoke of Don Francisco's books.

'Books?' he queried.

'Yes. I was told that there were quantities of quite valuable books here, but I haven't found them yet.'

Don Rodrigo smiled lazily. 'Who gave you this information?'

'The Englishman, Mr. Brunner.'

'Ah, you have seen him again?'

'Yes. This morning.' Averil was certainly not going to disclose that Connall Brunner had rescued her from a watery hole. 'I met him when I was walking across the fields. But Gonzalo says that most of the books were taken to Seville by the lawyers.'

'That seems surprising,' agreed Don Rodrigo.

'If they were to be valued, surely that could have been done here,' she suggested.

'Of course.' After a moment's pause, he added, 'It is possible that Don Francisco sold many of his collection himself. He may have needed the money.'

'I suppose that's possible,' she admitted. Yet she was casting about in her mind for some further way in which she could obtain Don Rodrigo's help in the matter of tracing the books.

'What else did Señor Brunner tell you about the Serena estate?' His voice cut across her thoughts.

'Nothing much. Only warned me not to be too impatient to settle the legal side in a hurry. He said it might take

19

quite some time.'

Don Rodrigo smiled and his dark eyes held warm, flattering lights. 'No doubt he is anxious that you should stay here for a long time. As indeed I am myself.'

Averil was not yet ready to yield to this Latin charm.

'What does he do? What work? He said he worked on the roads.'

'That is true. He is here to make preparations for a new road nearby, but work cannot start until later in the summer when the ground is dry. I have done my best to prevent this new road from coming where it is planned, but I have failed. You see, it is intended to cut right across the Serena estate, divide it in two almost.'

'Cut it in two? But won't that be a disaster?'

'It will not improve the estate.'

'But there is compensation, surely?'

He gave her a glance of admiration. 'You have a good business head. Where did you learn these things?'

'I've worked in my father's business and learned to use my common sense,' she replied, a trifle sharply. Did this handsome Spaniard believe that she was a brainless little idiot who could be hoodwinked and cheated out of the Serena inheritance?

'I know from my own experience how difficult these matters are,' he said slowly. 'In fact, the road also cuts across my own property and the compensation is still being argued about.'

'Then I ought to see the plans. Where would they be?'

He shook his head. 'I have no idea where Don Francisco's copy would be, but I could show you my set of drawings.'

'I'd like to see them as soon as possible.'

Don Rodrigo smiled. 'Then may I ask that you will come to my villa tonight for dinner? Some of my family live in Madrid—my mother, my two sisters—but one of my aunts runs the house when I am staying here.'

He was plainly telling her that she would be properly chaperoned if she accepted his invitation.

'That's very kind of you, Don Rodrigo. What time?'

'I will call for you at eight o'clock.'

As soon as he had gone, Averil inspected her wardrobe and chose a long mulberry-coloured skirt with a cream lace blouse. She had brought very little with her in the way of evening outfits, but if she needed one or two smart dresses, no doubt she could buy them in Seville or find the material to make them herself.

She was surprised to find that the Montilla house was some little distance from Don Rodrigo's estate.

'In England we're accustomed to farmhouses actually being part of the farm, but here the workers seem to live in the town or villages and go out to the fields every day.'

He smiled as he drove along a rough winding road. 'That is our tradition. In fact, in many other parts of Europe it is the same.'

'Where do your workpeople live?'

'In the village of Montilla. Some in the town of San-lucar.'

'It's a long way to travel every day.'

'Our people have a certain independence. They do not like to be chained to the place where they work.'

'Yet Don Francisco's villa is actually on his own land.'

Don Rodrigo shrugged. 'There is always an exception. That villa probably began as a small house for the foreman and then became enlarged.'

By now he was driving the car to the front of a house set in gardens and in a moment or two she was entering and being introduced to Doña Isabella, a small, plump woman with a pale face and the same kind of aquiline nose as Don Rodrigo's.

From her first glimpse Averil saw that the Montilla house was totally different from Don Francisco's shabby villa. The dining-room was panelled in dark wood and portraits and oil paintings decorated the walls. Pale orange lamps were set in brass holders in the corners and in the centre of the room a magnificent chandelier blazed and sparkled with brilliance.

The meal was protracted and Averil enjoyed several dishes new to her. Doña Isabella asked polite questions about the girl's visit to Spain and sometimes Don Rodrigo answered, partly in Spanish, for his aunt's grasp of English

21

was not very exact.

After coffee and brandy in the drawing-room, Don Rodrigo asked his aunt's permission to take Averil to his study to show her the plans of the road building.

'Ah, the road!' Doña Isabella exclaimed angrily. 'It is the work of the devil. Who would need a road if they have a horse to take them across the land?'

'But the road is for·cars and lorries,' Don Rodrigo replied gently. 'Horses do not go fast enough nowadays.'

'Tch! Speed!' his aunt snorted.

He conducted Averil across a wide hall and into a room along a corridor. Bookshelves, a massive desk and a typewriter indicated that this was Don Rodrigo's study. He unfolded the rolled-up drawings and began to point out the various properties through which the new road would run.

'Here is the new motorway from Seville to Cadiz. What is needed is a small piece to link the old road here with the motorway.'

'So the result is to cut the Serena estate into half with a busy road running between.' Averil traced with her finger where the proposed road touched Don Rodrigo's properties. 'I see it scarcely affects your estate. There's only a small corner cut off where it adjoins Don Francisco's.'

'That is so. We are perhaps more fortunate.'

'But who on earth designed it to go at that angle? Why couldn't it have come that way?' She pointed to a different part of the map.

'But that would have been worse,' declared her companion. 'All that land belongs to another of our neighbours.'

She turned to face him. 'More powerful than poor old Don Francisco, I assume?'

'Naturally, one must take into account the size and value of each estate.'

'I see.' She was thinking that the rich landowners had made sure that the road would disturb them as little as possible, while the smallest·estate, the Serena, was made almost unworkable.

'You must rest assured, *señorita*, that I will do all in my power to see that your interests are protected.'

'And the compensation? That can be hurried up?'

'Of course.' His hand was on her shoulder and she could feel its warmth through the thin lace blouse. 'There are matters that I could not have approached with Don Francisco, but now that you are here——'

'Not for myself. My great-aunt, remember,' she cut in.

'Yes, your great-aunt. Even so, it is more pleasure to be able to oblige a young and pretty girl than an old man—or even, perhaps, a middle-aged woman.'

He bent towards her and she felt the light kiss on her cheek. She moved away slightly as though to examine another part of the plan. She was still so close to him that she could feel his breath on her hair, but although she had drunk more wine at dinner than she was accustomed to, she was firmly in control of her senses. She did not intend to allow a pleasant dalliance with a handsome and romantic Spaniard to take precedence over the purpose of her visit to Spain.

It was satisfying, of course, to know that one had at least a single devoted admirer, if only temporary; apart from his probable usefulness in business matters, Don Rodrigo de Montilla was a man of undoubted charm and she would certainly find his company congenial during the time she was almost isolated in the marshy wetlands of Las Marismas where the winter and spring rains were only now subsiding.

She drew her finger across the proposed road on the plan in front of her and realised with a shock that she had already trodden on that firm stretch of ground only this morning when she had met Connall Brunner.

'Why is the Englishman here?' she asked. 'What does he do?'

She noticed a slight frown cross Don Rodrigo's face.

'He has no power. All he does is make sure that the machinery is handled properly. A British firm supplies some of the equipment.'

'But the Spanish Government plans where the roads must go?'

'Certainly.'

In that case, thought Averil, no help at all would come from the Englishman. He was no more than a medium for the operation of constructing the road. She must look to Don Rodrigo for assistance and was already convinced that he would give it.

Connall Brunner had not even told her this morning of the projected carving of the Serena estate in two, and she experienced a wave of resentment against his casual indifference to her situation in a foreign country. If she had not unwittingly stepped into the marshy pool, would he have ignored her, ridden by with no more than a curt *'Buenos dias'*? A question that could not now be answered.

She switched her thoughts away from Mr. Brunner and was relieved that on the drive home, Don Rodrigo made no further advances, but gravely wished her goodnight at the door of the Villa Serena.

'Until Tuesday,' he reminded her. 'The lawyer in Seville.'

'I'll remember,' she promised. The prospect of another visit to Seville compensated to some extent for the grey skies that loomed so often and so drearily over this unfrequented and surely untypical part of Spain.

CHAPTER TWO

Now that she had seen the road-planning map, Averil decided to walk again along that hardened track which apparently was to be the foundation of the new road.

Gonzalo seemed eager to accompany her, but she declined his offer. 'Probably you have plenty of work to do,' she told him with a hint of authority in her voice.

'*Si, señorita*,' he agreed, 'but there is little to do until the rains are over.'

'I'm glad to hear that they stop some time. When will that be?'

'Very soon.'

As she walked towards the track, she realised that it had not rained for two whole days, so even such small mercies were welcome.

The melon fields were on the opposite side of the projected road, as well as part of the small vineyard, but when she walked farther along, she found that only a tiny triangle of Don Rodrigo's land would be cut off.

She turned to retrace her steps and saw a horseman coming towards her. Naturally it would be Connall Brunner and now she regretted that she had come down here just at this time. He might think she had been hoping to meet him.

'Hello!' he greeted her when he was only a few yards away. 'I trust you're being more careful this morning where you step.'

'Perhaps I can't do better than walk along the new road, the one that's planned to cut across this property!'

He dismounted and draped his horse's reins over his arm. 'So you've been told about that project.'

'Since apparently you're concerned with it, why couldn't you have told me the truth yesterday when we met?'

He gave her a level look from his hazel eyes. 'I was not responsible for planning the road. I come along at the approximate date when work is supposed to start.'

25

'And when is that?' she asked.

'In about a week. Each morning I ride along this route to find out if the subsoil is dry enough to start laying the foundations. It's no good starting too soon or our equipment will sink into the mud. On the other hand, if we leave it too late, then we shan't have time to finish the road before the autumn.'

'Oh, I see. Apparently it does stop raining some time in these parts. Do you have a dry summer?'

He laughed. 'You must be prepared for a baking temperature if you're going to stay here very long. The ground cracks with the heat. Already over there on the right where there was a great sheet of water, you can see that there are dozens of islands and only small pools. In another month all the water will have dried out and the birds will have left.'

'What sort of birds, and where do they go?'

'In the winter ducks and geese by the hundred thousand, many other birds as well—storks who leave us in January to go north, little birds like goldfinches who stay here more or less permanently. Other birds come here for the summer months. Oh, I can assure you, Señorita Sanderson, that we're never lonely here.'

For a few moments Averil remained thoughtful. Then she said, 'You seem to like this marshy wilderness. Have you been here a long time?'

'Not staying here. I visited the district several times last summer when some preliminary work was being done on the road. Then I came at intervals during the autumn and early part of the winter and again I've been quite a few times since Christmas.'

'And in between you spend your time in the towns?'

'Certainly not. Usually on some precipitous mountain route elsewhere in Spain or hacking out a piece of new coastal road where nothing existed before except a mule track.'

Unconsciously, as he walked his horse slowly along the flat path, Averil had fallen into step beside him.

'I wish this new road didn't cut the Serena estate into two rather useless halves,' she said.

26

'It could be an advantage in the future, provided the land is properly worked and not neglected as it is now.'

'But how can I prevent that? I know nothing about vines or olives or melons. Gonzalo would take very little notice of my instructions.'

He gave her a sideways glance. 'Well, of course, I understand that you're here only for the purpose of straightening out the tangle of the inheritance. After that, you'll go home to England and your Aunt Tabitha or whoever she is will expect to receive large sums of money from her estate.'

'That's not quite the case,' she said with a touch of anger. 'Personally, I'm not interested in the money side of it at all. My great-aunt Freda is far more interested in the fact that Francisco has left her the property.'

'You mean that he thinks he has—or that your aunt thinks so. Remember there'll be a horde of distant relations to try to muscle in on anything that smells like money.'

'I've already been warned about that,' she retorted.

'By Don Rodrigo?' Connall laughed. 'I wouldn't put it past him that at some time or other, when he thinks you're sufficiently landed in the legal controversies, he'd offer to buy the Serena property.'

'But surely he has enough of his own?'

'Why should he miss the chance of getting an addition if he can get it at his own price?'

'Well, I don't know if Aunt Freda would consider selling,' she said dubiously, even though her common sense indicated that a reasonable offer might be better in the long run than a protracted legal battle ending in the possession of a run-down estate and a crumbling house unlikely to prove prosperous assets.

'You'd better think of all the possibilities,' he advised. 'Don't frown like that. You'll be prematurely aged in no time!'

'How can I help frowning when everyone seems to go out of their way to put difficulties in front of me?'

He gave a deep ripple of laughter. 'Have you been to Sanlucar?'

'An adroit change of subject,' she observed. 'No, I haven't yet had much time to explore the district.'

27

'Then I'm going there this afternoon. Care to accompany me?'

She hesitated for no particular reason, except that she did not want to appear as though she was jumping at the chance of an outing with this man who seemed to take delight in provoking her to anger.

'If you wait long enough,' he said with an ironic smile, 'I daresay Don Rodrigo will offer to take you there—so if you prefer——'

'I'll certainly come with you,' she answered firmly. 'Perhaps I can't then be accused of favouritism.'

But she realised at once that her phrase was not well chosen. He pounced immediately on her words.

'Favouritism? I'm hardly in the desperate position of needing favours where Don Rodrigo is concerned.'

'I didn't really mean that,' she protested.

His eyes, half veiled as he looked down at her, glinted with malicious amusement. 'Then I won't inquire too closely into what your intentions were.' He halted his horse. 'This is where I leave you. You're on Don Rodrigo's land, so take a good look at it as you go back along the track. Don't fall into an *ojo*.'

His horse had taken several paces before his rider called over his shoulder, 'I'll call for you at two-thirty. Why didn't you remind me?'

Averil stood there quivering with rage. 'Remind you? Why should I if it was such an unimportant matter?'

But she doubted whether he heard those last words, for the horse, probably impatient of dawdling, broke into a canter and Connall Brunner did not even turn his head to reply.

She was not at all sure whether she would make herself available for an afternoon's excursion with this arrogant Englishman who rode as he pleased across other people's land. Undoubtedly he would ride even more roughshod over other people's feelings.

She recalled herself to the fact that she was trespassing on Don Rodrigo's property, although since it was soon to become a public road, such an infringement hardly mattered.

And what did the Brunner man mean by not falling into

28

an *ojo*? That was the Spanish word for 'eye'. How could you fall into an eye? On arrival home she would search the dictionary and find if the word had another meaning.

In the patio of the villa Averil noticed a young girl brushing her long black hair. She glanced up as Averil passed, flinging aside the thick curtain of hair and smiled.

'*Buenos dias!*' the girl greeted her.

Averil returned the courtesy and walked on. Then she stopped and turned back. Surely she had seen that girl waiting at table last night at Don Rodrigo's.

'Do you work here?' she asked, imagining that there might be some sort of exchange system between the two houses.

'No. I live here—it is my home. I am Vanna and Gonzalo is my father.'

'Oh, I see. But you work in the house of Don Rodrigo?'

'Yes, *señorita*.' A delighted smile spread across the girl's features. 'It is like heaven to work in such a house—and for Don Rodrigo.' Vanna rolled her dark eyes in a gesture of extreme pleasure.

'But you live in his villa most of the time?'

'Certainly. I come here to visit when I have the time. Today, as you see, I wash my hair and dry it in the sun.'

Averil nodded. 'To be able to dry one's hair in the sunshine is a new experience after so much rain.'

Vanna laughed. 'But now the sun will shine every day until the winter comes again.'

As Averil reached the main door of the villa she saw Marta emerge from a side door leading to the patio and a moment later the sound of angry voices made her pause. Mother and daughter spoke so rapidly that Averil could not catch much of what was said, but she heard one sentence clearly—'Why did you let the *señorita* see you here in the patio?'

Vanna's reply was a torrent of phrases that Averil could not understand.

Averil went thoughtfully into the downstairs room that served as a sitting-room. It was poorly furnished with threadbare damask-covered chairs, tables covered by dark cloths to hide the dents and scratches. The curtains of dark red velvet had probably once held a lustrous glow, but were now faded and the pile perished in the folds. A single rug of some nondescript animal skin served only to call attention to the deplorable state of the marble floor, cracked and broken in many places.

Averil sighed as she settled in a chair for a few minutes. The villa would need an enormous amount of money spent on it to make it into a comfortable, well-cared-for home. But at this momnt her mind was more concerned with the incident of the girl Vanna, who was apparently the daughter of Gonzalo and Marta. But why shouldn't Averil have been allowed to see her on the girl's visits to her own home, even though she worked for Don Rodrigo only a short distance away?

After a short while when she judged that Marta and Vanna had perhaps settled their differences and calmed down, Averil went into the kitchen.

Marta was at the stove attending to the saucepans and she turned quickly at Averil's entrance. '*Señorita?*' she queried.

'I came to tell you that I'm going out this afternoon and may not be home to dinner,' Averil announced in her careful Spanish, speaking slowly so that Marta would have no excuse for pretending she had not understood.

Marta's dark eyes narrowed. 'You go out alone? Or with Don Rodrigo?'

'No. With someone else.' Averil's tone was curt, for she resented being catechised.

'Ah, of course. The Englishman.' Marta nodded and turned again to her pots on the stove. 'He likes girls and new faces, and an English girl makes him very pleased.'

'I would like my lunch at one o'clock, please,' Averil said firmly. 'Something light will do. An omelette, perhaps?'

Marta's dark face took on a sullen expression. 'In Spain we do not usually eat the lunch so early.'

For a moment Averil hesitated. She was not accustomed to ordering other people and now she was on the verge of yielding, but the stubborn expression in Marta's eyes seemed to indicate to Averil that this trivial incident was to be a trial of strength. If she surrendered now she would find it difficult to regain any kind of authority in the household.

'I'm aware of the usual hours for Spanish meals,' she said, 'but I would still like something to eat at one o' clock.'

Marta nodded, her eyes veiled, and Averil walked quickly out of the kitchen before any further controversy could arise.

Yet when she reached her room and opened the large mahogany wardrobe to decide what clothes she would wear for the afternoon excursion with Connall Brunner, she paused to consider by what right she was trying to exert her authority over the late Don Francisco's household.

She had no status as a relative, she was merely a representative of her great-aunt Freda, the new owner when all the formalities had been settled. So Averil now justified herself in taking some of the control into her own hands, if only for the ultimate sake of her great-aunt. All the same, she wondered if Marta would pay the slightest attention to her request.

At five minutes to one Averil presented herself in the dining-room and was gratified to find that a cloth had been laid and cutlery and condiments were on the table. At a quarter past one she was still waiting and was about to storm into the kitchen when one of the young maids who worked in the house came along with a tray of covered dishes. The girl set them down before Averil and scuttled out of the room as though pursued by a hostile animal.

The meal was tolerable, although Averil suspected that Marta had prepared the items and then deliberately kept Averil waiting while the soup cooled and the omelette toughened. Still, perhaps it could be counted a minor triumph of wills.

Connall Brunner arrived punctually and escorted her to his car. 'As I warned you,' he told her, 'I don't run to the magnificence of Don Rodrigo.'

'I'm not used to luxury,' she replied swiftly. 'My father always has some antiquated old car that makes alarming noises but usually gets us to our destination.'

Connall laughed. 'Antiquated, yes. But without the noises, I hope.'

On the journey he pointed out the dwindling lakes that

left islands of vivid green where new grass was springing up almost overnight. Farther away the silver curves of the Guadalquivir river shimmered in the sunlight and the air was full of birds in flocks or flying in twos and threes.

'The terns and coots are already arriving.' He indicated a jostling crowd of grey, white and black creatures trying to settle on a small piece of land still surrounded by large pools.

She turned to glance at his profile as he steered the car along a road that twisted and turned to avoid the swampy places. 'You do really like this part of Spain, don't you?' she murmured quietly.

'And you don't really see how anyone in their senses could admit to such an odd taste?'

'It's a contrast to other parts of Spain, certainly.'

'You don't understand what a varied country this penin- sula is. Mountains, deserts, miles of sandy beaches that have only been discovered and developed in the past few years. But there are little towns that haven't changed much in the last hundred years, valleys tucked away in folds be- tween the mountains and, of course, this wasteland of water and dunes and wide open skies that stretch to the horizon.'

Averil shivered slightly. 'I doubt if I shall ever come to rejoice in the landscape. No colour, no romance.'

'You must be blind!' he exclaimed. He stopped the car. 'Look over there! Where else would you see such brilliant patches of green——?'

'Probably treacherous bogs where people fall in,' she in- terrupted.

'Or blue sky with racing white clouds?'

'Most of the time I've spent here the sky has been grey.'

He shook his head and started the car again. 'You've no feeling for the land!' he accused roughly. 'I suppose at home you live in a town with pavements and supermarkets and plenty of shop-windows to gaze in.'

'Yes, I do,' she agreed, striving to keep calm. 'But if you're so attracted to a desolate slice of country, why do you want to run a gash across it with your new road?'

'M'm, I thought we'd get around to that subject. Good question—if only I could answer it. I've already explained

32

that I have no say at all in the line or direction of the roads. The local authorities decide.'

'In spite of protests from landowners?' she queried.

A smile curved his mouth. 'Do protests in our own country always succeed in preventing the ruin of an area of natural beauty or scenic value?

'Well, perhaps in the end my aunt will receive handsome compensation for the damage.'

He was now driving into a small town and made no reply.

'Sanlucar?' she queried.

'Sanlucar de Barrameda, to be precise. There's another Sanlucar farther inland near Seville, so you mustn't confuse the two.'

He was driving down a main wide avenue lined with houses of one or two storeys set in gardens. At the foot was a wide expanse of estuary where the Guadalquivir met the Atlantic.

'I have to make a call here,' Connall explained. 'Will you wait in the car or stroll about? I shan't be more than about a quarter of an hour.'

He had stopped outside a yard cluttered with building materials, bricks, bags of cement and drainpipes stacked in rows.

'I'll walk about for a while,' she decided.

'Don't lose yourself,' he warned her.

'Or fall into a keyhole?' she jeered in return. She had discovered that the word *ojo* about which he had cautioned her this morning also meant 'keyhole' as well as 'eye', but she could still find no sense in his meaning.

Now he flung back his head and laughed. 'Keyhole? Do you think you're Alice in Wonderland?'

'Then what is an *ojo*?' she demanded.

This question caused him even more merriment. 'I'm delighted that you should find my conversation so extremely funny.' She put all the acid she could muster into her tone.

'Trust the English for ludicrous literal translations,' he said, still laughing. 'You need a better dictionary. In due course I'll show you an *ojo* and you'll be glad I warned you.'

He gave her no time to reply, for he marched off across the yard and through a doorway.

Of all the conceited, arrogant, ill-mannered, overbearing specimens of bumptious males she had ever had the bad luck to meet, this man Brunner was undoubtedly the worst! A road navvy, that's what he was. In fact, a real navvy would probably be insulted at being likened to Connall Brunner. Why on earth she had ever allowed herself to come with him today was beyond belief. No doubt she could have discovered some other way of visiting this little town. More than that, she would find some other method of returning home. There would be a bus or taxi.

She walked briskly along by the shore, but the only vehicles she saw were small handcarts or tradesman's vans, an occasional bicycle and several horse-drawn open cabs.

She approached the driver of one of these last conveyances, a middle-aged coachman with dark skin and lively black eyes.

No, he told her, he did not undertake long journeys. Only from the railway station to hotels or for a ride round the town.

'How far is the railway station?' she asked. There might be a train that would take her part of the way, but it seemed that the line went to Jerez de la Frontera and then made a winding detour inland on its way to Seville.

Averil hesitated, uncertain of her next move.

'You would like me to drive you around the town?' the coachman asked.

She nodded. Having taken up his time with questions, it seemed unfair not to use his services. As she settled herself in the ancient vehicle, she began to laugh, imagining Connall Brunner's face when he discovered that she was missing. He would naturally conclude that she had lost herself or fallen into the sea. Once or twice she glanced behind to see if his car might be following, but evidently he had not finished his business at the building yard.

She gave herself up for at least the time being to the enjoyment of this leisurely way of seeing a small town with its inns on the estuary bank, a modest hotel halfway up a low hill.

'Is that a castle up there?' she asked, glimpsing walls that appeared against the skyline.

'Si, señorita. I take you there.'

On the same ridge as the castle were several attractive buildings, a church, a tower decorated with coloured tiles, one or two handsome houses.

'Perhaps I could get out here and explore,' suggested Averil to her driver.

As he slowed his horse to a stop, a car whizzed past and halted a few yards ahead.

Averil needed no second sight to realise that this was Connall Brunner catching up with her. She affected not to notice him, but chatted amiably to the coach driver. Then Connall was at her elbow, interrupting her conversation with quick, fluent Spanish. He handed the man some peseta notes and there was an exchange of smiles and thanks.

She regretted that she had stepped out on to the road, for if she had stayed in the cab, Connall could not have dismissed it in this high-handed fashion. Now, to her chagrin, she watched the driver turn his horse and trot away down the road.

'I suppose you became tired of walking,' Connall said in the silkiest tone imaginable.

'Not in the least,' she returned coolly, controlling the inward fury that threatened to explode into violent anger. 'I happen to think that a horse's pace is probably the best way to travel about a town.'

'I must remember that.'

Reluctantly she had walked beside him to his car and now he held open the door with an elaborately gallant burlesque gesture.

'If you could condescend to ride in my humble boneshaker,' but she cut his words short.

'Oh, please spare me the play-acting,' she said tersely.

He drove slowly towards the castle. 'Do you want to explore the ruins?' he queried.

'Now that I'm here, I suppose I might as well.' She knew her voice sounded ungracious and her awareness of the fact that she had certainly behaved stupidly added to her discomfiture. 'Who knows when I shall have another chance

35

of being in Sanlucar?'

He gave a snort of laughter. 'I doubt if I shall invite you again to Sanlucar, but there is always the handsome Don Rodrigo. Perhaps you would be willing to wait ten minutes for him without dashing off on your own in a gypsy's cab.'

'Gypsy?'

'Yes, a number of them live in the ruins of the castle, your driver probably among them.'

Her resentment forgotten, she said more eagerly, 'Then I'd like to see.'

As they walked over the tussocky grass towards the ruined walls, Connall admonished her, 'Please don't go wandering around on your own. When these people see girls as fair-haired as you, they lure them into secret passages and then ask for enormous ransoms.'

'How dramatic!' she jeered. 'With you as my protector I'm quite sure no such terrible fate could happen to me.'

'Don't rely on that! I might prove to be untrustworthy.'

She gave him a sharp glance, but the face he turned towards her was blandly innocent of malice or mischief.

'Naturally you know your own character much better than I do.'

He made no reply, for three small children had clambered out of a hole in the ruined walls and came running towards Connall.

'*Dulces! Dulces!*' they shouted, clinging to Connall's legs.

'No sweets today,' he told them, smiling at their downcast faces. Then he disengaged himself from their clutches and told them to stand in a line like soldiers. He took out a few small coins and tossed them to each child in turn. 'That's the lot, all you get today.'

As soon as the two boys and the girl saw that the distribution of largesse was finished, they shouted '*Gracias*', but were already streaking off down the slopes towards the town.

'Do they always come out to meet strangers?' Averil asked, 'or do they know you?'

He laughed. 'They usually think that the pockets of people who roam about here are lined with pesetas or sweets, but I do know those three. Let's go and meet their mum.'

Averil was surprised at the degree of comfort and homeliness achieved by the several families living in the remains of the castle. Strong roofs had been erected to keep out the rain and while the interiors of the dwellings were dim through lack of light, there were bunks covered with brightly coloured rugs and blankets. Each family apparently did its own cooking on fires outside its own quarters and an appetising aroma came from some of the black iron pots suspended over glowing embers.

Connall spoke to a couple of the women, dark-eyed and brown-skinned, one of whom gave Averil some piercing glances. Gently she lifted Averil's hand and peered at the palm, but Averil as gently withdrew it. She shook her head at the woman and smiled as disarmingly as she could. She had no desire to hear her fortune told in the presence of Connall.

'She'll read your future,' suggested Connall now with a malicious gleam in his eyes.

'Another time. Not now.'

When they left the castle ruins and walked down the slope, Averil looked back. 'Apart from a few wisps of smoke, you'd never imagine that whole families lived so snugly inside,' she remarked.

'Rent-free, too,' added Connall. 'But gypsies everywhere have always learned how to make the best of the worst conditions.'

'Usually they'll put up with discomfort for the sake of their freedom.'

'Freedom?' he echoed. 'A debased word. One man's freedom can be another man's chains.'

'Surely you've chosen your own kind of freedom, roaming about one country and another telling them how to make their own roads.'

'I wonder,' he murmured. They had now reached the place where he had left the car, only to find the three gypsy children sitting on the bonnet.

Connall shooed them off with peremptory Spanish exclamations and they fled, shrieking with laughter.

He took Averil to a small restaurant with a café-terrace on the first floor facing the wide estuary and beyond, the silken shimmering sea, gilded by the setting sun as it dipped below the horizon.

While he studied the menu, handwritten in red ink and including items completely unfamiliar to Averil, he ordered glasses of *manzanilla,* the pale dry sherry which Connall told her was actually made in Sanlucar.

'The food will take a little time to prepare,' he said. 'We're here rather early for dinner, but you can keep your hunger at bay with these small snacks of fried liver and olives and cheese and so on.'

'*Tapas,*' she said. 'Kind of Spanish hors d'oeuvres. Yes, I sampled some of different sorts when I went to Seville.'

'Ah, with the handsome Don Rodrigo. Please don't let his shadow fall between us on this pleasant evening when two is enough without an intrusive third party.'

She grinned at him over the rim of her glass. 'Sorry. I wasn't intending to remind you of the only other man whom I've met since I came here.'

He gave her a long measured glance. Then he changed the subject abruptly. 'This little town, Sanlucar, has had quite a history. Did you know that Columbus set out from here on his third voyage and Magellan started here his voyage round the world. At one time or another famous people have come to live here. Also, a number of the wine firms have their *bodegas* here as well as in Jerez.'

Now it was quite dark and the restaurant proprietor brought small lamps to place on brackets at the corners of the terrace and along the balustrade. They provided enough light to distinguish what one might be eating, but they cast ever-changing mysterious shadows on the faces of the diners.

Averil watched in fascination as the conflicting lights played on her companion's strong straight nose, his narrow cheeks and the curves between forehead and eyelids. He was gazing out across the dark water and she guessed he was taking no notice of her scrutiny although acutely aware of it.

He turned swiftly to meet her gaze and she was surprised

38

to feel slightly discomfited as though she had been caught spying.

'You're very silent,' he commented. 'Thinking precious thoughts?'

She recovered some of her poise. 'Not exactly. Only that I met Gonzalo's daughter today.' She plunged into the first topic that entered her head. 'A girl named Vanna.'

His interest was apparently keenly aroused. 'Oh, yes, Vanna. That's short for Giovanna.' He smiled and put his elbows on the table and leaned towards Averil. 'Quite a girl! Naturally she enjoys working in Don Rodrigo's house much better than she would like scouring and polishing and scrubbing in your villa.'

'How old would she be? Eighteen? Nineteen?'

'Eighteen and a half. I gave her a shawl for her birthday just before last Christmas.'

Averil digested this piece of information while he continued, 'If she can keep out of the clutches of Don Rodrigo, she might make something of herself. She has intelligence as well as looks. She told me the other day that Don Rodrigo has promised her a place in his Madrid household.'

'Oh, so she might leave here?'

He grunted. 'If she really believes that yarn, she's more foolish than I thought.'

For a few moments there was silence. Then Averil said, 'I'm not sure that much scouring and polishing takes place at all in the villa where I'm living. Besides Marta, there are two young girls, but the house is not only shabby, but un-cared-for. Even without much money, it could look much more pleasant.'

Connall nodded. 'A clever scheme of Gonzalo's. You see, he sends his own daughter out to work elsewhere, while he then employs two other girls, both of whom have to eat at your expense—or your aunt's—and in the meantime, Vanna is kept at Don Rodrigo's and earns a little dress money.'

'In some ways, Gonzalo seems to have a good business sense,' replied Averil. 'I wish I could believe that he also does his best for the Serena estate.'

'He'll never do more than his best for Gonzalo.'

The first course was now served, a tunny fish soup which included red mullet and chick peas, followed after an interval by medallions of veal cooked in wine sauce with mushrooms and artichokes.

'Delicious!' was Averil's verdict. She was on the point of apologising for her absurd behaviour this afternoon when she had attempted to dodge Connall while he transacted his business affair. 'To think I might have missed such a treat if I——' she began, but the proprietor came to offer a new bottle of wine to Connall. Just as well, she thought, not to give Connall a further opportunity of gloating over trivial pranks.

When the meal was finished, Connall showed no signs of wanting to leave. He stretched out his long legs and lit a cigar. Across the estuary pinpoints of light were dotted along the shore and on this side in Sanlucar clusters of lights illumined the quays.

Averil was silent, relishing the peace of the evening, punctuated only by the murmur of voices from other diners on the terrace or an occasional shout of greeting from someone down in the street below.

Then Connall broke abruptly into her mood of indolence.

'Are you engaged or—expecting to be married soon or anything like that?'

The suddenness of the question jarred her into resentment. 'Is it any business of yours?' she demanded ungraciously. 'Actually no. Not engaged or flinging myself headlong into marriage—or *anything like that*.' She stressed those last words with mocking emphasis.

He tapped the ash off his cigar with deliberation. 'M'm. I'm surprised. I imagined there might be someone special at home and you'd be longing to get back to him as soon as possible.'

She stared at him stonily. 'Remember it was you who asked me to come here with you today. I didn't invite myself, but you seem in a hurry to send me packing back to England. Why?'

He did not look at her but continued to gaze across the terrace. 'I just thought that if you had a real attraction back home, you'd be proof against the handsome Don and his

40

attentions.'

'Warning me? I'm twenty and old enough not to fall into a man's arms because he escorts me to the bus stop or sees me home after a dance. My young sister Dinah is at the romantic age and goes through a succession of boy-friends like a knife through butter.'

'But you're different?'

'Of course. I intend to take my time over marriage—I'm not yet on the shelf—and I'm not jumping at the offer of some man's heart and hand just to be a housekeeper, cook his meals and darn his clothes.'

Connall laughed softly. 'Emancipated ideas, I see. Not for you the pots and pans of domestic life, but perhaps a successful career.'

She shook her head. 'I'm not that ambitious. I doubt if I've very much talent except in a small way. If it interests you, I'll admit that I was quite pleased to escape for a while from the humdrum life of working for my father in his business.'

'So you did expect to meet adventure or at least taste a few delights in a foreign country?'

'Naturally,' she declared. 'Now, after your lengthy quizzing session, let me have my turn. Are you engaged or married—or *anything like that*?'

'Why do you want to know?'

'For the same reasons that you asked me all those questions. I'm just naturally inquisitive. I enjoy poking and prying into other people's affairs.'

Now he turned towards her and she saw his shadowed face in the flickering lamplight. 'If you're going to flare up so easily, some man in the future is going to have a hell of a time cooling you down.'

'You've ignored my questions.' For no reason that she knew it was suddenly important to her to know his present status.

'No,' he said slowly. 'Tying myself down in a neat little detached on a new estate and living with the kitchen units and the mortgage doesn't appeal to me. I'm a born roamer and in my kind of job you need to be footloose.'

'And fancy free, of course,' she finished for him before he

41

could say anything further.

'And fancy free, as you say,' he agreed. 'Perhaps maybe I'm not the marrying kind.'

Now it was her turn to laugh. 'How many men have said those very words!' she bubbled with glee, 'only to find themselves marching down the aisle with a radiant bride on their arm! I wish you luck in retaining your bachelor state.'

'It seems we can agree on one point. You'll be choosy when it comes to a husband. I'll be content to rub along as an elderly bachelor, godfather to my friends' children and remembering who is old enough to want a cricket bat next birthday.'

He finished his cigar, the proprietor approached with the bill and in a few moments Averil rose to leave the restaurant. Connall pulled a chair out of the way for her and guided her with his arm around her shoulders. There was only the slightest pressure of his fingers on her upper arm, but it was enough to lift her emotions to an unexpected level. In the car on the way home she reminded herself that this unexpectedly intimate conversation had served a definite purpose. In the darkness she smiled at her thoughts. Connall Brunner certainly lost no time in warning off any girl who might acquire delusions about his intentions.

As he drove into the courtyard of the Villa Serena, it occurred to her to ask him, 'What excuse did you give that coach-driver when you so rudely snatched me away from his cab?'

He swung the car in a half circle before replying.

'I told him that you were a very dear friend of mine who was in my charge and that you were in the habit of wandering off in strange towns if you had the chance. So I was glad to find you again.'

She held her breath for an instant before she let it out again in a gasp of white-hot anger. 'In other words, that I was an escaped loony!'

'Not exactly that! Just unpredictable, shall we say?'

He leaned across to open the door on her side of the car, but she thrust his arm aside and scrambled out unaided.

'Thank you, Mr. Brunner, for the ride—and the dinner —and your contemptuous notions about me.'

She ran through the open front door of the villa and upstairs to her room before anyone could notice her homecoming or ask questions. She flung herself on the bed and tried to control her temper, clenching her fists and pounding them on the black and red quilt. What right had he to insult her with his taunts, probe into her personal affairs? She did not believe for an instant that he had really spoken of her as mentally unbalanced to a coach-driver, but he had to take the opportunity of ridiculing her.

She could hear voices down in the courtyard and then Connall's laugh. Oh, yes, no doubt he was retailing to Gonzalo his account of the afternoon and evening with the green English girl. She looked around the room for some handy object to throw out of the window and break up such a rewarding conversation, but the next moment there was the sound of a car driving off.

Relief flooded over her and she remembered that in a couple of days' time Don Rodrigo would be taking her to Seville. Her tempestuous anger died with the anticipation of a day in the company of a man, civilised and urbane, who knew how to treat women.

CHAPTER THREE

THE outing with Connall Brunner to Sanlucar and his bluntly expressed low opinion of her inspired a new determination in Averil. So he thought she was a quitter, an inexperienced representative of an absent owner who was merely on the look-out for an easy income from other people's labour.

She called Gonzalo and Marta for a discussion next morning. First she explained that until matters were decided otherwise, then she was the authority empowered to act for her great-aunt.

Next, she demanded to see all the accounts of the past year.

'This estate could be much more prosperous,' she told Gonzalo. 'The land is neglected and not tended properly.'

Gonzalo gave her a crooked smile. 'You do not understand, *señorita*,' he muttered. 'What can we do when no money is spent? Also, there is the road that will come. We have no heart for making the estate prosperous.'

'On the contrary,' retorted Averil, 'the coming of the road makes it still more important that Serena should be in good shape. There should be more compensation for a fertile farm than one that has obviously been allowed to ~n down. Then there is also the villa. How many girls work ı you, Marta?'

'Two—Lola and Nita.'

'And also the elderly woman whom I have seen in the kitchen?'

'That is Ana. She is a widow and——' Marta stopped suddenly, apprehension in her dark eyes.

'She is Marta's cousin,' explained Gonzalo, 'and she has no home, so we must take her in.'

Averil stared at the man in astonishment. It was on the tip of her tongue to demand angrily if she were expected to give board and lodging to various other relatives of Gonzalo and Marta if they had nowhere else to turn. But she remembered that in Spain there were much closer family ties than in her own country and possibly Ana had come some years earlier and been given permission by Don Francisco.

So now she nodded her agreement. 'Then with three people to help you, Marta, even if Ana cannot do much, I expect this villa much better kept in the future. Many of the rooms are dusty and the furniture in bad condition. If necessary, some of the rooms could be shut up and their contents distributed among the rooms that are more often used.'

To her surprise, Averil saw a slow smile creep over Marta's dark-skinned features.

'*Si, señorita.* I will attend to it.'

Averil hoped that Marta meant what she promised. Could it be that a brief show of authority after so much lack of supervision might be a welcome change to the household? Don Francisco had evidently left the domestic affairs entirely in the hands of Gonzalo and his wife and they had become slack.

'You and I, Marta, will go round the house tomorrow and see what needs to be done.' Averil turned towards Gonzalo. 'If you will bring me the books tonight, Gonzalo, perhaps we could study them together?'

'The books?' he echoed, consternation on his face.

'Yes, the accounts. Surely you must write down what is spent and what money comes in.'

Relief flooded over his features. '*Si, si, señorita.* I understand.'

It occurred to her some time afterwards that her casual reference to 'books' had made him believe that she meant the missing books belonging to Don Francisco's extensive collection.

The first sign that evidently her demands for better discipline were being taken seriously came later in the morning before lunch, when Averil went upstairs to her room. At the end of the passage two girls, evidently Lola and Nita, were lugging a large chest of drawers out of one room.

'Why are you moving the furniture yourselves?' Averil asked. 'It's too heavy for girls. You should get the men to help you.'

The two girls fluttered confusedly around the chest and a final push succeeded only in wedging it across the doorway.

'Look!' explained Averil. 'If you took out all the drawers first, it would be easier.'

She helped the two to push the chest halfway back into the room and they followed her instructions, setting the drawers in a pile one on top of the other.

Averil stared around her at the contents of the room. Evidently this was the best bedroom, for it was more than twice as large as her own. Obviously at some time in the past it had been enlarged, or two rooms had been made into one, for there were three windows, one leading to a balcony.

But it was the quantity of furniture crammed into the room that surprised Averil. A large carved bed in rosewood was surrounded by tables, wardrobes, dressing chests, armchairs and stools, so that there was scarcely space to move about. The room was like a furniture store. So this was where so many pieces had been piled up.

'Whose room is this?' she asked Lola.

The girl reddened and bowed her head. 'Señor Gonzalo and Señora Marta,' she whispered.

Averil had already guessed that. She now realised that when she had first been taken on a tour of inspection, only a few of the rooms had been disclosed to her. Naturally she had not wished to pry into the personal rooms of the foreman and his wife. At the time Marta had vaguely indicated that some of the rooms were either occupied by the maids or were empty and shut up.

'Where are you taking this chest of drawers?' Averil now asked one of the girls.

'To that room,' the girl answered, pointing to one next to Averil's own bedroom.

'Leave it for the time being and go downstairs. I will have it attended to later.'

The two girls were only too glad to scuttle away and avoid further questioning.

Averil paused, wondering how she was to tackle this situation. Lola and Nita would soon spill the news to Marta that the English *señorita* was asking questions and poking about in other people's rooms.

She decided to wait until after lunch, but if she delayed longer than that, much of the extra furniture would be moved out of this crowded bedroom. The threat of to-morrow's complete inspection had evidently alerted Marta into speedy action.

'We will speak privately,' Averil announced when she entered the kitchen in the early afternoon. She would spare Marta's pride in front of two giggling girls.

Averil led the way into the sitting-room. 'May I ask which bedroom you and your husband use, Marta? I am not prying, but I would like to know.'

'The one in the corner.'

Marta's answer was almost ludicrous. Her words sounded as though she had to sleep cooped up in a small boxroom.

'You mean the large room facing the patio, with a balcony?'

Marta nodded.

'Then why on earth is it so cluttered up with furniture?' continued Averil. 'Surely you and Gonzalo can't move in there without knocking against a chair or table or chest of drawers.'

'Gonzalo said it would be best to put some of the furniture in there so that we could look after it.'

'Do you mean so that it could not be taken away? Out of the house by someone?'

Marta nodded, eagerly grasping this solution.

'Who?'

The woman shrugged. 'I don't know. The lawyers, per-haps. Or some of Don Francisco's family when they heard he was dead.'

Averil remained thoughtful for a few moments. 'I see. But did you occupy the room in Don Francisco's time?'

'Oh, yes. He told us to use whatever rooms we wanted. He slept in a little room at the end of the passage.'

Averil sighed. Marta might possibly be lying all the time, yet it seemed that an old man might make this kindly gesture, since he needed only the barest of creature com-forts and apparently did not entertain.

Averil smiled at Marta. 'Then tomorrow we will sort out what is not really necessary in your room and arrange it in some of the other rooms. But we'll have the men to help us.'

Marta's eyes showed fear. 'Oh, no, not Gonzalo! I mean he is usually busy with the estate.'

'There are several other men and boys who work here. A couple of strong lads can shift the pieces about for us.'

After dinner Gonzalo came to the sitting-room, bringing with him a handful of assorted papers, receipts, invoices and the like.

'You said you wanted to see the accounts,' he began, in one of his surly moods.

'Is this all you have? Don't you enter the items in a notebook?'

Gonzalo shook his head. 'No need. If I order, the bill comes in. I pay and that is finished.'

'But there are wages to pay the men. Surely you keep a record of those?'

'Oh, no. The men know what they will earn. Each week I pay them and that is all.'

Averil considered this rough-and-ready method of book-keeping. It was certainly primitive by any standards.

'Well, we'd better look at these bills and accounts you have there.'

But she could make little sense of any of them. Lacking a knowledge of the basic principles of running such an estate, she could not understand the abbreviations, the scrawling handwriting, the additions and subtractions.

She could feel Gonzalo's sense of triumph, but she was determined that he would not have all his own way.

'Yes,' she said, as she handed back the creased and crumpled documents. 'I will buy an account book when I go to Seville and then I'll show you how to do simple accounts.'

Gonzalo's smile faded. 'No, señorita, I am too old to learn such college notions.'

'Nonsense! You can read and write. Even your daughter Vanna could do the simple sums that is all I want. You see, Gonzalo, we have to convince the lawyers that the estate is properly conducted.' This was a shot in the dark, for she guessed that the lawyers would scarcely care about the state

48

of the Serena's finances as long as they carried out their duties in a proper legal manner and were eventually paid accordingly.

'Oh,' muttered Gonzalo, apparently a little impressed by this view. 'But I don't write well.'

'No matter,' was Averil's reply. 'We shall get along.'

She waited a moment to see it he would mention the subject of the furniture all piled into one room and what would be his glib explanation. She took the plunge herself.

'I shall want a couple of your men tomorrow for about an hour or so. There is furniture to be carried about.'

His dark face was immobile. 'Marta has told me that you want us to move out of our room.'

'No, not that. Not yet, anyway. Later on, perhaps, but I want to rearrange some of the furniture throughout the house. In any case, surely you and Marta will be glad of the chance to get rid of some of it. You haven't space to move.'

A momentary flicker came into his eyes and she concluded that her words 'get rid of it' had struck a responsive spark. It was almost certain that a number of items in Don Francisco's household had probably been sold off at some time or other by Gonzalo. It was becoming obvious to Averil why so many articles were stacked in the one room over which Gonzalo and Marta had control.

When next day Averil made her promised complete tour of the entire villa she discovered several surprises. Some of the rooms on the upper floor were almost bare, but one which had first to be unlocked by Marta held some interesting sculptures, a few paintings, two or three rugs and an exquisite writing desk inlaid with excellent marquetry.

Averil noted down on her list everything interesting or not. If it were true that the lawyers' representatives had come here and made an inventory since Don Francisco's death, then she might be able to compare her own list with the official entries.

Lola and Nita had already been set the task of cleaning some of the rooms.

'Thoroughly, please,' cautioned Averil. 'The floors washed, the wall and ceilings dusted. Then we will move furniture into wherever seems best.'

Ana's room was already spotlessly clean, although rather meagerly furnished. 'She keeps it clean herself,' explained Marta.

Averil mentally added a good mark in favour of the elderly widow, Marta's cousin, who appreciated a roof over her head and a seat at the kitchen table by making herself responsible for her own room.

By the end of the day Averil was as tired as the rest of the household, but she was convinced that she had accomplished something more than the spring-cleaning of a few rooms. She had assumed authority, even if she had only the most slender right to it, and by doing so, established a warmer and more human atmosphere with Marta and the others. In fact, Marta seemed actually pleased to be bossed. Gonzalo, of course, was different, a harder nut to crack and wrapped in a masculine pride far above the petty domestic details that rightly were the concern of the women.

'Tomorrow I am going to Seville with Don Rodrigo,' Averil told Marta late in the evening. 'It's possible that I may stay the night with his friends there, so don't wait up for me.'

'*Si, señorita.* I hope that everything will come right at the lawyers. Also, I will see that Lola and Nita clean out all the other rooms we have not yet done. When you come home, everything shall be tidy and good.'

'Thank you, Marta.' Averil smiled her appreciation.

She packed a small overnight bag and was ready next morning when Don Rodrigo called.

'I hear you've been turning the villa upside down,' he said when he had driven a short distance.

Averil laughed. 'Such news travels fast, apparently! I thought it was time to give the place a good shake-up. It needs a lot of money spent on it to make it really elegant, but something can be done to make it more habitable than it is now.'

'I fear that Marta won't like it if you take the reins out of her hands.'

'On the contrary, she has been so surprised at my arrogant, bullying ways that she has been very co-operative indeed. Unless, of course, she is only acting like that to fool me.'

Rodrigo gave her a sideways glance. 'You are not yet very experienced in the character of the Spanish people.' He sighed deeply. 'It is our pride. So often we kick our toes against a brick wall rather than humble ourselves.'

Averil was silent, puzzling as to her companion's exact meaning. Was he trying to warn her off making improvements at the Villa Serena?

'And how did you like Sanlucar?' he asked after a few moments.

She smiled. 'I liked it very much. It seemed a warm, friendly little town.'

'And your companion? Was he also warm and friendly?'

'Sometimes.'

'Ah, then there were moments when you disapproved of his behaviour?' Rodrigo seized eagerly on the idea of what she had left unsaid.

'One doesn't have to approve all the time of everything a friend—or acquaintance—may do or say. Life would be very dull if there were nothing to argue about.'

He laughed deep in his throat. 'Then I'm glad you argued with the Englishman. I should be very unhappy if he found favour with you.'

'Oh, I don't know him well enough to talk about favouring him. I gather he's here only for short spells of time to examine the roadway and then he'll go to some other project elsewhere.'

He leaned slightly towards her. 'That is where I have the advantage over him. I live here, close to your villa. I hope we shall become very good friends.'

'For the short time that I expect to remain here,' she answered. 'I'm here only for the time it takes to settle the affairs of the estate with the lawyer.'

Although he was looking straight ahead, Averil was sure that the slight smile that curved his lips was echoing the same disbelief that Connall had expressed when he spoke of the slow progress in legal matters. So evidently Don Rodrigo would not be displeased if she were forced to stay in Spain for a lengthy period.

The appointment at the lawyers' office was not until the late afternoon and Don Rodrigo suggested lunch first at one of the restaurants in the centre of Seville.

51

'I take it that your friends here have been warned that I'm being dumped on them for the night,' she said, as he scanned the menu. 'Where do they live?'

He glanced at her over the top of the menu. His eyes caressed her, but she could not see his mouth. 'Of course I have informed them. They have an apartment in the Plaza de Santa Cruz, one of the most beautiful of the smaller squares in Seville.'

The lawyers' office was in the business quarter and after the long leisurely lunch, Don Rodrigo suggested that Averil might like to walk in the park for a while.

'I should like that,' she agreed. 'Some fresh air before we smell the dusty documents of the legal offices.'

One part of the park was filled with children, some in the charge of smart nursemaids, others playing happily under the watchful eye of their mothers.

A great cloud of white fantail pigeons seemed to descend on Averil from nowhere and for a moment she was startled as they perched on her shoulders, her arms and hands.

'Oh, I wish I'd brought my camera with me,' lamented Don Rodrigo. 'This would make such a charming photograph.'

'Evidently I should have brought with me a bag of bird food,' she said, but the flock fluttered off in the direction of two children who were scattering seeds.

In the lawyers' office Averil produced her small sheet of paper on which she had written down numerous questions to ask.

The notary, Señor Navarro, glanced briefly at the items, but before answering her queries, removed his spectacles, polished them, replaced them on his nose and leaned forward across his desk.

'I regret that I have some news for you, *señorita*, that may be a disappointment.'

He paused and she said impatiently, 'Yes?'

'There is another claimant to the estate. A niece of the late Don Francisco.'

'But I thought that Don Francisco definitely decided by his will that the property should come to my great-aunt Freda,' protested Averil.

'Indeed, so,' agreed Señor Navarro, 'but there are certain

circumstances in which the will can be contested, especially by a close relative.'

'What is the exact relationship of the niece?' asked Don Rodrigo.

'She is the daughter of Don Francisco's sister. Her name is Renata Bonaventa.'

'Is she claiming for herself alone or for others in the family?'

'At present, as far as I can say, she claims the entire estate for herself alone. She is not married and she is an only child.'

There was silence for a few moments in the office where files and packets of documents were stacked on the shelves. How many other inheritances had been tugged this way and that over the years, thought Averil, and here was all their history wrapped up in affidavits and court evidence.

'Is it possible that some compromise, some settlement might be agreed upon?' queried Don Rodrigo.

Averil was immediately up in arms over this apparently yielding attitude of Don Rodrigo.

'I shall not give up easily,' she declared warmly. 'This Señorita Renata will have to prove her claim, just as I'm trying to prove my aunt's.'

'Exactly,' assented the lawyer calmly. 'In the meantime I have arranged for you to meet the young lady.'

'Perhaps it would be better if we did not meet her,' Don Rodrigo put in. 'Then we would be dealing with an impersonal claimant.'

Señor Navarro pursed his lips. 'That is one aspect, certainly, but the *señorita* very much desires to meet the English girl—and, of course, yourself, Don Rodrigo.'

'How do I come into it?'

'Naturally, I have explained that your estates are close by the Serena property and that you are helping Señorita Averil in the legal steps necessary. So, with your permission, I have arranged for you both to meet Señorita Renata in one of the hotels here.'

'Does she live in Seville?' asked Averil.

'No, in Cadiz. She has come specially today in order to meet you both.'

'When is the appointment?' asked Averil.

53

'Tomorrow at one o'clock at the Hotel Salamanca. Do you agree?'

Don Rodrigo looked questioningly at Averil, who agreed immediately. 'Yes, I think it better to meet my opponent.'

'Now, these queries,' continued the lawyer. 'To some I may have the answers and others may take a little time.'

'First, there is the question of money to pay the staff at the Villa Serena. Gonzalo claims that he has not been paid for several months and there is no more money coming in for produce.'

'Of course, I am allowed to advance wages for the domestic staff, but I must look into the matter and see at which date payments were stopped.'

'Yes,' replied Averil, 'I understand that. Then there is the matter of the books. I believe that Don Rodrigo had a fairly valuable library, but few books seem to have remained at the villa and Gonzalo tells me that one of your assistants took them away to be valued.'

The lawyer's face became concerned. 'The books? But if we sent a valuer, the books would not be removed from the villa. There must be some mistake there. Perhaps a further search?'

'That can certainly be done,' interposed Don Rodrigo.

Averil glanced across at him, but he merely smiled at her. 'There is another point,' she began, turning to the lawyer. 'Compensation for the new piece of road that will cut across the estate. Are you handling that?'

'I think that has already been paid into the estate,' he answered slowly. 'But I will check it for you.'

'I see. So if it's been paid, there's no more to come?'

'I'm not sure that we ourselves have received our compensation,' Don Rodrigo put in, 'so possibly there will be something further for the Serena estate.'

There were several other queries, most of which Señor Navarro could answer, and now Averil felt that although some matters had been straightened out, she had come up against a brick wall with this other claimant's sudden appearance.

As Don Rodrigo rose to leave, he said casually, 'Perhaps you could also arrange for a sum of money to be handed to Señorita Averil. Enough to pay for her own personal ex-

54

penses while she is staying here in Spain.'

Averil was not looking in the lawyer's direction as she too rose, but she heard his hesitant words, 'Ah, but I cannot——' followed by a hasty, 'Yes, yes, señor. Of course I will do as you wish.'

In the car as Don Rodrigo drove away from the office, Averil congratulated him on such a happy thought of asking for some money for her.

'The only thing that worries me is that if I should lose the entire estate—that is, the estate on my great-aunt's behalf—and this Renata girl is successful, then I suppose I should have to pay the money back?'

He laughed. 'Please don't worry about such trifling amounts. The Serena estate can afford a few hundred pesetas.'

He arrived in the Plaza de Santa Cruz and stopped outside a tall house on one side of the square.

Don Rodrigo's friends were enthusiastic in their welcome of both him and the English girl he had brought with him. Averil was introduced to Señora Rabell and her two daughters and then put in charge of a maid who showed her to her room, handsomely furnished with a huge bed piled high with billowing coverings. An enormous wardrobe of dark wood inlaid with Moorish patterns was large enough to hide oneself in, let alone hold the single dress she had brought with her.

The maid pointed out the bathroom adjoining and began to unpack Averil's modest bag. No doubt the girl was more accustomed to guests who possessed more elaborate brushes and combs and travelled with an extensive collection of beautiful clothes.

When the maid had gone, Averil tried to pull aside the heavy curtains drawn across the windows. She wanted to see if her room looked over the square with its tiny garden in the centre, and was delighted to find that this was so. The lamps on elaborately ornamental brackets attached to the cross illumined the flowers that clustered around the metal plinth below. As she watched, a couple strolled along the path and paused below the cross. They were young and stood there, arms entwined, in a dreaming world of their own. As the young man bent to kiss the girl's upturned face,

55

Averil let the curtain fall from her grasp. She had no right to intrude on that delicate little scene. The *plaza* was made for lovers in the darkness.

Unbidden, the thought of Connall Brunner entered her mind as she stood there. Had he declared his aversion to marriage because someone had broken his heart in the past? Or was he merely afraid for the future?

She thrust the notion aside. She had other concerns to dwell upon rather than idle curiosity about Connall.

The two Rabell daughters were extremely attentive to Don Rodrigo, Averil noticed during dinner. They were polite enough to include her in the conversation occasionally, but it was obvious that his visits were much appreciated.

They had both dressed elaborately in their best, with necklaces to flash against their creamy skins, and Averil felt like a sober sparrow in the patterned terylene dress she had brought because it did not easily crease.

Señora Rabell divided her attention between Don Rodrigo and Averil, asking a question here and there about the progress of the legal affairs of the Serena estate.

'I knew Don Francisco quite well,' she told Averil. 'But he shut himself away too much and left others in charge. Perhaps he should have married your aunt and been happy with her.'

'Evidently he did not want to marry anyone else,' murmured Averil.

'A pity. There were others who would have been glad to share a home with him.'

Averil glanced at the older woman in surprise. 'Even in so unattractive a spot as the Serena?'

Now Don Rodrigo's attention was caught. 'Unattractive? Perhaps that is so, for it is the reason why some of my own family prefer to live in Madrid.'

'You are quite wrong,' asserted Señora Rabell. 'It is not the surroundings that influence women. They make a *home* with a man they love. No matter if the country around is depressing, then there is all the more reason to make the *cortijo* pleasant.'

They were laudable sentiments that the Señora expressed, but Averil was uncertain whether an English girl, her aunt Freda or anyone else, would have been glad to settle down so comfortably in the Villa Serena, even though, no doubt, in the early days it had not been as neglected as it now appeared to be. Would either of the Rabell daughters be so eager to remove themselves from the mild gaieties of Seville to marry Don Rodrigo de Montilla and bury themselves in the heart of a wet wilderness?

Would Averil herself consent to live permanently in such a place even with a husband to whom she was devoted? The transient thought was amusing, as well as futile, for the possibility would never arise. She was here for so short a duration that it was unlikely she would have time to fall in love. And with whom? Don Rodrigo who had houses elsewhere in Spain? Connall Brunner who had so determinedly impressed upon her that he was not the marrying kind?

She now became aware that the dinner-table chatter had ceased and the faces of her companions were turned expectantly towards her.

'You were smiling,' Don Rodrigo told Averil. 'At your thoughts or at something one of us said?'

'I apologise. I—I——'

'There is no need for apologies,' broke in Señora Rabell. 'All girls must lose themselves in dreaming sometimes.'

After the lengthy meal ended, Don Rodrigo suggested that he should take Averil out for a short walk so that she could see the city by night.

The two girls showed disappointment in their faces and one exclaimed, 'But, Rodrigo, we have not seen you for a long time until now.'

Her mother said quickly, 'Señorita Sanderson has not had the chance of walking in Seville, and you have seen the city many times when it is lighted.'

When Averil and Don Rodrigo left the house and walked in the direction of the main avenue near the Cathedral, she said tentatively, 'I didn't wish to take you away from your friends. I mean it wasn't really necessary to bring me out if you wanted to stay and talk.'

He had linked her arm in his own and now put his other hand over her wrist. 'Why should I forgo the pleasure of escorting you for the sake of those two foolish girls and their idle chatter?'

'How flattering the Spaniards can be!' she said, and was immediately abashed because she had spoken that thought aloud.

'But if it is not flattery, but sincerity, what then? Since I first met you, I have found you a charming and delightful companion.'

Averil was saved the necessity of replying, for he had conducted her to a more dimly-lit street from where the full blaze of the floodlit Cathedral dazzled the eyes. Against the blue-black sky, the beautiful tower of La Giralda—the weather-vane—was bathed in a rose-red glow, a superbly artistic touch, for the tower was the only remaining part of the original Moorish mosque.

'How beautiful it all is,' breathed Averil, feeling the tense excitement evoked by this lovely spectacle, while at the foot of the huge Cathedral dozens of people strolled or hurried, unmindful of the splendour above their heads.

Rodrigo escorted her to the Plaza de España, where again the circular line of buildings punctuated by towers and spires was bathed in a rosy glow that left the numerous arches in mysterious shadow and picked out the Venetian bridges that arched across the circular ribbon of lake.

'Seville is a dramatic city,' Averil remarked as she and her companion strolled among the crowds, thinner here in this vast space than they were in the narrower streets.

'Dramatic?' he echoed. 'Yes, perhaps it is. Our Andalusian cities, Seville, Cordoba, Granada, have retained much of their ancient capacity for enjoyment, while Madrid regards itself very soberly, like a parent who must restrain his excited children.'

'I haven't been to the other cities,' she murmured, 'but I must try to see Granada while I'm here.'

'You must also see Seville during Holy Week and afterwards at the Feria. This is the peak of the whole year for gaiety.'

When they left the Plaza with its sparkling intensity of light, Don Rodrigo, as though to display the city's contrasts, plunged her into a dark street, through a gateway and along narrow, twisting streets of white houses, with black wrought-iron balconies and grilles. There was no moon, only a star-filled sky and ornamental lamps on brackets at the corners of streets. Waves of orange blossom scent were carried on the breeze and there were few sounds to break the curiously hushed atmosphere. It was like an enchanted fairyland, she thought, a magic dream from which one would awake suddenly and be surrounded by a laughing, chattering crowd.

But this shattering of the dream did not happen, for soon Averil saw they had reached the small *plaza* where Señora Rabell and her family lived.

Rodrigo slowed his pace as they walked through the tiny garden with its wrought-iron cross and neatly-kept box hedges.

'I think you have bewitched me, Averil,' he said huskily, putting his arms around her.

'Not me. It's the night and Seville and——' she began to make excuses, but his lips clamped down firmly on hers and stopped her protests. Even as he kissed her lingeringly and lovingly, on her mouth, her cheeks, her temples, she wondered apprehensively if someone unseen behind a window somewhere were watching, as she had earlier this evening glimpsed the embrace of another couple. Perhaps even one or both of the Rabell girls? What would they think?

'I've fallen completely in love with you,' she heard Rodrigo saying, then whispering endearments in Spanish. 'You must also love me, for I cannot bear to be refused.'

'But, Rodrigo, I've known you only for so short a time,' she murmured, her face against his cheek, for he was holding her so tightly that she could not move. At the back of her mind she was asking whether she really wanted to move away from his embrace.

'What does time matter? An hour, a day, a week? I knew I should love you when I first saw you. Did you not feel the same for me?'

She was at a loss to know how to answer with discretion and tact. These swift Spanish tactics in lovemaking had taken her by surprise, although inwardly she realised that she might have expected sooner or later that Don Rodrigo would declare a passion that she suspected had assailed him many times before in his life.

'Perhaps English girls don't allow themselves to—to hope for too much—no, I mean——' she broke off, flound-

59

ering. She was giving him quite the wrong impression.

'I understand entirely. In your climate, you become cold and distant like a star, but a star has warmth as well as radiance, and I shall warm you into life. Oh, my flower, it will be my happiness to cherish you and——'

'Please, Rodrigo, not so fast. You must give me time to know you.' He was racing on and taking far too much for granted.

He laughed down into her face. 'Yes, you shall know me. Together we will have such a magical life that everyone will envy us. Other men will look at me with angry jealousy in their eyes because they did not meet you first. The Englishman most of all.'

A dagger of ice seemed to stab Averil. The Englishman. Connall would laugh himself silly if he could see her in her present situation. He would crow 'I told you so!' and congratulate himself yet again that he was not the marrying kind. She pulled herself away now from Rodrigo and he demanded immediately, 'What is wrong? What is the matter?'

'Perhaps we should go indoors before we are locked out,' she said lightly.

He laughed such possibilities away. 'That will not happen. Come, kiss me again.'

'No, Rodrigo, please, not now. I'm rather tired. It's been a long day.'

At once he was solicitous. 'Of course, my darling. I am a very selfish man. We will return now, for I shall look forward to tomorrow.' He kept his arm firmly about her waist as they strolled towards the Rabells' house.

'We must remember that tomorrow we have to meet this young lady who is claiming the Serena estate,' she reminded him.

'Ah, yes, the niece. She will have no effect upon us. She will be brushed aside like a fly.'

That remark penetrated Averil's sleepiness. No effect upon *us*? Rodrigo's thoughts seemed to have leapt into a distant but entirely settled future that included herself.

'We'd better wait until we see her,' she said quietly. 'She may be quite formidable.'

CHAPTER FOUR

In the Hotel Salamanca next day, Averil could not yet determine whether Señorita Renata Bonaventa would prove to be a formidable opponent or not. She was certainly strikingly beautiful. With her dark glossy hair and deep brown eyes, she was slightly taller than the average Spanish girl and moved with an easy elegance that caused heads to turn in admiration.

She subjected Averil to a prolonged scrutiny that stopped just short of an offensive stare, then gave a sudden smile.

'The matter is most easily settled,' she said in Spanish, and while Averil could understand this opening, she needed Don Rodrigo to translate and interpret for her when the Spanish girl really warmed to the subject.

'The great-aunt is of no account,' she declared. 'She is not a relative. It would be different if she had married my uncle, Don Francisco, of course.'

'In that case I probably would not be here trying to straighten out the legal side on behalf of my great-aunt,' retorted Averil with politeness, but with a subtle warmth of spirit which made Rodrigo glance at her with encouragement.

'Quite so. But I am a blood relation, the daughter of his sister,' continued Renata.

'Yet his will left everything, or at least all the estate, to my great-aunt.'

Renata's scornful expression dismissed wills and the wishes of the deceased as of no account.

'Of no importance,' she said briefly. Then she smiled with tremendous charm, a dazzling radiance that swept over Don Rodrigo as well as Averil. 'But we shall be friends, naturally. It would be wrong to quarrel over such a poor trifle.'

Averil remained silent for a few moments. If the Serena estate in its present condition could be called a 'poor trifle', and that was certainly not far from the truth, it might be an easy way out of all the difficulties to let this new claimant establish her title to the property and then be responsible for all the upkeep. In that way, Averil thought, her great-aunt Freda would not be throwing away yet more good money after bad.

She deemed it more prudent, however, not to mention these ideas. Let Renata find out in her own way if she really wanted to be saddled with such a property. In any case, Averil had no authority to hand over what apparently belonged to her own relative.

Over lunch Rodrigo played the perfect host and once or twice Averil caught a glimpse from Renata that indicated more than a mild interest in Averil's Spanish friend. Other matters were discussed and no one made any further reference to the thorny problems that had arisen.

'You must come to Cadiz and see my home,' invited Renata.

'With pleasure,' returned Averil, believing it to be one of those vague proposals that people so often make without any intention of making a definite arrangement. But in this case she was wrong, for Renata opened a handsome diary with a tooled leather binding and her gold pencil poised, asked Averil when would be a convenient date.

'I'm not sure of arrangements,' answered Averil tentatively, unwilling to bind herself to dates quite so hastily.

'There is Holy Week in a few days,' interposed Don Rodrigo, extricating her, 'and Averil will need to see some of the processions in Seville.'

'But ours in Cadiz are just as marvellous and exciting,' objected Renata. 'It would work out well to come next week and see our festivities.'

In the end Averil avoided making a definite promise, but agreed that some arrangement might be made later by correspondence.

Renata produced a visiting card embossed with all her family names, a whole string—Renata Maria Bernardina de Campaña y Alqueria de Monestero Bonaventa—and an address in Cadiz.

It was early evening when Rodrigo and Averil finally

bade goodbye to their new acquaintance and started the journey home.

As he drove through the outskirts of Seville Rodrigo sighed heavily. 'What an extraordinary girl! I felt as though she were a great eagle hovering over me, waiting to devour me.'

Averil laughed. 'I found her most overpowering,' she admitted. 'If she's really serious about her claim, I shall never have enough strength to oppose her.'

'That would be a pity,' he returned. 'You must not let flashing eyes and a voluble tongue defeat you so easily.'

He had arranged with Señora Rabell that he and Averil would not wait for dinner at the house, but eat at a restaurant somewhere on the way.

'But why not here?' she had queried. 'We do not see you very often, and now you are running home so quickly.'

Rodrigo had replied that staying for dinner would nean that he and Averil would not arrive back home until well after midnight.

Señora Rabell had shrugged her disbelief that this was any kind of valid reason. 'How many times have you been out at three, four, five in the morning?'

But Rodrigo was apparently determined not to stay, and when he presently stopped at a restaurant at a fork in the road, Averil began to understand his purpose.

The restaurant was small, but the food excellent and Rodrigo was evidently well known to the proprietor, who greeted him with jovial remarks and smiles.

Averil was surprised to find that after a pre-dinner dry sherry, Rodrigo ordered an Oloroso with his meal.

'I thought this was a wine to drink after dinner,' she said. 'Like Madeira, for instance.'

Rodrigo laughed. 'Nonsense! Spaniards drink sherry with all kinds of meals, and why not, when we have such a good range of our own wines?'

'It may be all right for you—and all Spaniards—but such potent sherry is rather heady for me. I'm not used to drinking so much.'

'Nonsense!' he murmured in a low, warm tone. 'You must have something to restore your energies after our encounter with the lady Renata.'

He refilled her glass and held his own up to the light. 'Oloroso, a dark and elegant wine, fit for happy and personal occasions.'

Averil had little option but to raise her glass with his while he murmured, 'You are so beautiful tonight, my love.'

There were long waits between courses and it was a shock to Averil when she glanced at her watch and saw that the time was past eleven o'clock. So much for trying to arrive home before midnight. The other diners in the restaurant had long since finished and Averil and Rodrigo had the place to themselves.

'Another bottle?' queried the proprietor.

'No more for me,' Averil said with determination. She could not tell Rodrigo how much he should drink, but secretly hoped that his driving would not be erratic when they resumed their journey.

He smiled at her and reached for her hand across the table. 'There is a coldness about you tonight, my jewel. Have I made you angry?'

'Of course not,' she replied lightly. 'Nothing to be angry about.'

'Then sip a little wine with me like a charming companion.' He leaned forward and kissed her forehead. 'There is no need to be alarmed by spectators. We are alone.'

In the corner of the room by the service door stood the proprietor, a beaming smile on his dark features. When he caught Averil's glance, he turned aside and busied himself with wiping a row of glasses.

'We ought to go soon,' she suggested. 'It's really quite late.'

'Not before I give you a toast. To the English girl who has captured my heart!'

'I can't drink a toast to myself,' she protested with a smile. 'Or is it someone else you're referring to? Some other girl whom you once met in Seville?'

His face immediately darkened. 'Please do not jest with me. I am very serious indeed. You are the only girl who has ever entered my life and whom I cannot bear to lose.'

In other circumstances Averil would have made some

light retort that his words were the kind of pretty speech that comes so easily to a Latin tongue, but she was anxious to resume the journey home. So now she smiled and raised her glass.

Another half hour went by before Rodrigo was ready to leave, but as soon as he had driven a short distance from the inn, he stopped the car.

'My dearest, you are so cold tonight towards me,' he whispered as he folded her into his arms in a stifling embrace. 'I thought the good food and wine would warm you into life, but I was wrong. What has made you so distant?'

'Nothing, except that I don't usually rush into—into falling in love.'

He laughed softly, his mouth against her cheek. Then he moved his face a few inches away. 'Perhaps I am glad to hear you say that, for I know that when you do fall in love it will be for ever. You are not like girls who delight to break men's hearts for the pleasure of it. So I am very pleased, because I know that eventually you will fall in love with me. How lucky I am!'

Averil could make no answer to this flowery and confident forecast, for he was kissing her with more ardour than she enjoyed. Even as his lips sought her mouth, her neck, her closed eyes, she reflected that such a heady display of affection was an entirely new experience. She remembered her sister Dinah's words—'swept off her feet by any amount of handsome Spaniards . . .' Well, to some extent it was pleasing enough to be escorted by a handsome Spaniard, but she was not yet swept off her feet by Rodrigo's attentions.

When at last he now released her after a final passionate kiss that was slow to end, he settled himself at the wheel and started the car. It was then than a vagrant thought strayed into Averil's mind. If Connall Brunner showered such kisses upon her, what would be her reaction? In the darkness, she smiled a secret smile. She was never likely to know the answer to that futile question.

At the door of the Villa Serena, Rodrigo helped her to alight, then raised her hand to his lips with a formality that surprised her. Was he afraid in case someone were watching? She let herself in the house quietly, for the outer doors were apparently never locked at night, but Gonzalo shuffled along the passage from the kitchen, nodded and muttered '*Buenas noches*' as she ascended the stairs to her room.

For the moment she was too tired to dwell on the events of the last two days, the appearance of a rival claimant to the estate or the ardent attentions of Rodrigo. Tomorrow she would deal with her problems. Yet when she was in bed, sleep, tantalisingly, would not come. On that last part of the journey home she had been dozing off most of the time, perhaps partly due to the wine at dinner. Now she was wide awake and even her eyes refused to remain closed as she stared at the ceiling. She rebuked herself for seeming to encourage Don Rodrigo, yet it was difficult to strike the balance between being a too easy conquest and adopting a cold English politeness that might prove even more irresistible to a man of his type. As a neighbour to the estate she wanted to keep on good terms with him, if only for the sake of her great-aunt Freda, but she must avoid giving her the impression that she was eager for romance.

By early morning she was surprised that she had slept so soundly after all. She rose and, as soon as she had breakfasted, went out for a walk. The sun shone out of a clear blue sky without the slightest hint of rain, and even after an absence of only two days, it seemed to Averil that more of the large pools on the meadows either side of the road had dried up still further and grass was taking the place of water.

The air was invigorating, she thought, or perhaps it was the contrast between this almost limitless area with its wide horizons, and the streets of Seville, intriguing and charming though they were.

She paused to look at a flock of terns trying to settle on a series of floating islands in what had been only a few days ago a sheet of water. For the first time since she had arrived she experienced the attraction of this part of Spain. The desolation of a watery world, endless tussocks dotting a vast plain, and grey rain-sodden skies had given way to spring and a rapid transformation.

In her new enthusiasm she walked on for some distance down the road where there was little traffic other than the occasional car or small van. After some time she turned back, for there were no side roads where one might take a short cut. Almost immediately a car was driving towards her and she stepped aside, for the road was fairly narrow.

The driver slowed and leaned out. 'Good morning. How was Seville?'

Connall Brunner stopped, although she would have been ready to return a cool 'Good morning' and continue on her way home.

'Seville was most attractive,' she answered.

'And the handsome Don Rodrigo?'

'What about him?' she queried.

'Well, was he at his most attractive, too?'

She shrugged. 'We had all the legal business to attend to. There's a new problem. Another person claims the estate.'

'Who?'

'A young woman, niece of Don Francisco.' She glanced quickly at his face. 'Don't say that you told me so. That there would be rivals to try to get their share.'

Bland innocence was all that she saw, except for an interested expression in his eyes. He opened the door of the car. 'Come in and tell me all about it.'

She had never intended to do anything of the sort, but because he was English and therefore easy to talk to, at least as far as language went, she grasped the chance of sharing her problems. There was another reason, too, at the back of her mind. He would certainly not imagine that she wanted to flirt with him, for he had warned her off in the most decisive manner.

She told him about the lovely Renata from Cadiz and the girl's complete assurance that she would succeed in inheriting.

'She's amazingly beautiful,' she added with a sly glance at Connall. 'She lives in Cadiz, and I have her address.'

'Really? What are you expecting me to do? Intercede for you?'

'I thought you might like to make her acquaintance on your own behalf.'

'What has Don Rodrigo done to you? Stolen your heart? And now you can't bear it unless you fix me up with a prospective bride?'

'I don't go in for matchmaking,' she said with mock aloofness. 'In any case, as you said, you're not the marrying kind, so you could enjoy a happy friendship with a lovely Spanish girl. Or do you know too many already?'

'I'll bear this new possibility in mind. Now we were saying—about Don Rodrigo—where did he take you to amuse you in Seville—apart from the lawyer's office?'

'Oh, we walked about in the Maria Luisa park, but we were staying with his friends, Señora Rabell and her daughters.'

'Yes, those two. No man is safe from their clutches.'

'Speaking from experience?' she queried.

'Yes, indeed. They came to stay with Rodrigo's aunt, Doña Isabella, and I met them once. They frightened me to death and I fled in cowardly terror. Too honey-sweet for me. I was terrified that before I knew what was happening, one or other would haul me before the registrar and I'd be going through a civil marriage ceremony.'

Averil laughed. 'Tosh! I don't believe a word of it! The boot would be on the other foot. You probably flirted with both of them.'

'Well, my past is my own affair. Tell me about Don Rodrigo's progress with you.'

'We left Seville and came home last night, that's all. We stopped at an inn for dinner and ate some very pleasant food and drank Oloroso——'

'Oloroso?' he echoed, then spluttered into raucous laughter.

'What's so funny?' she demanded.

'Oloroso! Dear Averil,' he turned towards her with the air of an instructor teaching a favourite pupil, 'I shall have to caution you about the various kinds of sherries. Oloroso is considered the wine to be drunk on honeymoons, according to the vintners, or more generally, before making amorous advances.' Connall was laughing again. 'Trust Don Rodrigo to try that ploy!'

'I'll be extremely careful next time I drink sherry,' she

said icily, annoyed with him for ridiculing Don Rodrigo.

'Of course you can't be expected to know these fine distinctions. But I'm relieved to know that you arrived home safely.'

His glance conveyed that his curiosity was not yet satisfied, but she was not going to blab to Connall about another man's amorous attentions.

'Let me take you towards the junction of this road,' he suggested, 'and then I'll take you back home to the villa.'

'If it weren't quite such a long distance, I'd say that I prefer to walk back.'

'Please yourself, but don't blame me for sore feet.'

'What's exciting at the road junction?' she asked.

'You'll see when we get there.'

A gang of men were working at what was apparently to be the new junction of the road that would eventually cut across the Serena property. Drainpipes were being fixed in trenches and farther along new trenches were being dug by an earth-moving machine. More men were actually watching the machine doing its mechanical digging than were actually needed to operate and Connall spoke to one, evidently in charge of the others.

'They've been so used to digging trenches and holes the hard way with picks and shovels that they're all fascinated by a machine that does the work for them,' Connall told Averil when he returned to her near the car.

'Is this the first time one has been used here?' she asked.

'Not exactly. There have been others in various districts, but this is a special pattern made by my firm for use in such difficult country as this, where in a few weeks the soil goes from almost liquid mud to iron-hard baked earth.'

He spent a few minutes in conversation with the foreman, consulting plans and large grubby sheets of drawings.

'So far, so good,' Connall said when he was back in the car. 'I have to check up every day on how much work is done, so that if we do fall behind schedule, we know how much longer the job will take.'

On the journey home, he suddenly pointed across the plain.

'Look, Averil!—snowy egrets. White birds about the

size of a heron and with a plume of feathers on top.'

She saw a cloud of white birds apparently feeding on a small grassy island.

'When there's enough grazing for the cattle to come on the marshes, the egrets often ride on the bulls between the horns, and that's a very pretty sight,' explained Connall.

'Are they here all the year round,' Averil asked, 'or only in the spring?'

'All the year round. They don't migrate like many of the other kinds, but during the spring and summer you'll see all sorts of birds. Farther to the west there is the wildlife preserve, the Coto Doñana, a refuge for birds and animals from the greed of modern civilization. I must take you there some time.'

When he was in this gentle mood of pointing out the attractions of the district, Averil could forgive his waspish remarks, his acid jeers. He had stopped the car so that she could see the egrets and she turned towards him with a smile.

'You really love this part of Spain, don't you?'

When he turned towards her, her pulse gave an unexpected jump at the flickering expression in his eyes.

'Yes, I do,' he said after a pause, still looking at her. 'I'd been interested in it for a long time, but I had no opportunity of coming. It's a place that grows on one. At first you may think it's dreary, especially in the rainy season, but for the rest of the year, there's so much variety, everything happens so quickly that every day is a surprise.'

She smiled and turned her head away, looking down in her lap. 'I appreciate the wildlife here, but I don't think I could ever become even slightly enthusiastic about the district.'

'But you've been here only two or three weeks. Even in that time, you've seen changes.'

'True, but——'

'Oh, of course if all you want of Spain is sea, sun and sand and a sixteen-storey matchbox lump of hotel, you should have gone to the resorts on the Costa del Sol,' he said testily.

'That would scarcely have been much help to my great-

70

aunt,' she retorted. 'I didn't come here for a holiday.'

'No? Certainly it must have been hard work for you to visit the notary in Seville, even though Don Rodrigo was at hand to smooth your path and cheer you up with a little wining and dining.'

'What else do you expect me to do? Dig the land or prune the vines or lift the melons or whatever it is that has to be done? I should soon get black looks from Gonzalo if I interfered.'

'Oh, you'd never have the patience to do any of those jobs skilfully enough,' he returned, starting the car.

Her mouth set in a rebellious fashion. 'I'm like the boy who was asked if he could play the violin. He said he'd never tried. That goes for me, too.'

'Violin-playing?'

She gave an exasperated sigh. 'What's the use of talking to you at all, when you can only reply with nonsense?'

For a moment or two he was silent, although a smile lurked around his lips. Then he said softly, almost humbly, 'If you'll tell me the kind of things that Don Rodrigo says to you, then I'll mend my ways and follow his example. There's a fair offer.'

'Fair nothing!' she snapped. 'You never lose a chance of ridiculing me.'

'Dear Averil, I'm in the most sincere and serious mood. I really do want to improve my uncouth manners.'

'You've plenty of scope there,' she pointed out with satisfaction.

'Then you should help me, not rail at me in your school-marm manner.'

For a few moments she stared straight ahead, then turned her head quickly to observe him and found that he was in danger of doubling up over the wheel in convulsive laughter.

'That's right, laugh at me now!' she burst out angrily. Then she, too, was forced to laugh. The whole argument had degenerated into triviality.

By now they were nearly home and as Connall drove into the patio he said, 'Don't get me wrong this time, but you'd have much more fun if you rode a horse around these parts.'

71

She flushed and murmured in a low tone, 'I've never ridden.'

'All right, I'll teach you,' he volunteered.

'I'm sorry, Connall, but I—I don't think I'm brave enough. Horses terrify me.'

He looked across at her for a few seconds, then picked up her hand and held it in his warm clasp. 'What about a donkey? Or have you too much pride to be seen on a Spanish *burro*?'

She hesitated. 'I don't know. I realise that I'm missing chances of exploring the district, but——'

'If you could ride, even a donkey, you could accompany Gonzalo sometimes and see that he attends to the planting and hoeing at the right times.'

She smiled. 'I don't believe he'd welcome me on his rounds.'

'It's up to you to make him accept you as the boss. Assert yourself the way you've already begun to do in the house.'

'Oh, you know that already?' she queried.

'Certainly. Vanna is a useful spy, since she has contact with both your house and Don Rodrigo's.'

'So you listen to spy tales,' she said quietly with a smile. 'I must remember that.'

'Vanna said that you'd turned the household upside down in a few minutes and had everyone scurrying about altering the arrangement of furniture, cleaning out rooms and so on.'

She told Connall of the extraordinary collection of furniture piled in the bedroom occupied by Gonzalo and Marta.

'I had some shifted into other rooms.'

'You realise that they've undoubtedly sold some of the best pieces and that by hoarding a number of other items in the room they used themselves, they would be able to hide them from your prying eyes and then dispose of them when they chose.'

Averil shook her head. 'I think you're quite wrong. I don't believe they would be so dishonest. I've always understood that Spaniards are not like that. They respect other people's property.'

'On the whole, that's true. It just happens that in Gon-

72

zalo you have the exception. In many ways he shouldn't be blamed. For years Don Francisco neglected the place, land, house, everything, and Gonzalo had to do the best he could. It's hardly surprising that he saw ways of putting a few extra pesetas into his own pocket.'

Averil sighed. 'What an inheritance! I wonder sometimes if my great-aunt Freda wouldn't be better off renouncing her claim and letting this girl Renata take over.'

'What!' he almost yelled. 'Let the first upstart claimant have it handed to her on a plate? Really, I thought you were made of tougher stuff than that. In any case, if you did just that, this Renata girl would probably have to fight her way through a tangle of other relatives, distant cousins, in-laws and so on. I wouldn't be surprised if Don Francisco foresaw all that and therefore he willed the property to his old sweetheart to avoid all the value being whittled away in lawyers' costs.'

She alighted from the car. 'Would you like to stay to lunch?' She had no idea why she invited him. His conversation was either scolding her for being a quitter or else he was ridiculing her in that derisory manner that pricked her composure.

If she had been half hoping that he might decline, his immediate acceptance extinguished that idea.

Averil went into the kitchen to tell Martha that he would be lunching here and Connall had followed her. The two young maids, Lola and Nita, immediately stopped what they were doing and began to giggle and whisper and cast sly smiles at Connall over their shoulders. He merely stared at them, a genial smile on his lips, but when Averil turned to leave the kitchen, he called out something in Spanish which made the two girls giggle afresh. Averil decided it would be beneath her own dignity to ask him for a translation.

At lunch he told her details about Cadiz. 'If you like, I'll take you there for a quick look round before you commit yourself to visiting this Renata woman.'

'Can you spare the time?' she asked mischievously, eyeing him over the rim of her wineglass.

'No,' he answered crisply. 'But while you're here, I've

73

taken it upon myself, as your fellow-countryman—you understand,' he paused to give her a mock gallant bow—'to cast a guardian eye on your roamings around the country. Cadiz is a city that has seen much history, as you probably know, and it would alarm me if you were caught up in a kidnapping or something of the sort.'

Furious anger struggled with her desire to laugh at his ridiculous notions. 'I think I can safely look after myself on a visit to Cadiz,' she said coldly. 'I don't expect to be thrown into a dungeon.'

He shrugged. 'Have it your own way.'

After the meal she accompanied him to the patio and the stables where the horses and donkeys were kept. 'Will you condescend to try a donkey-ride tomorrow?' he asked.

'It's a long time since that treat of a donkey-ride on the sands came my way,' she answered mockingly. 'But I'll try to make time.'

'If you're going to adopt that attitude, I shall make sure that you have an obstinate animal who will give you a very uncomfortable ride,' he threatened.

'I'm sure that you're always willing to add to my discomfort.'

He stood there, grinning at her, his hands in the pockets of his sand-coloured trousers. 'Why I don't take you by the shoulders and shake you enough to make your teeth rattle, I don't know!'

As she returned his gaze, a devil of mischief welled up in her, challenging him to carry out his latest threat. She saw his hands begin to withdraw from his pockets and although she still faced him, she took an involuntary step backwards.

The sound of a car entering the patio caused Averil to turn her head sharply and Don Rodrigo eased himself out of his car with agile grace.

The two men eyed each other, Don Rodrigo with a haughtily inquiring stare, Connall with more an amused expression in his hazel eyes.

After the briefest of formal greetings, Rodrigo said, 'I came, Averil, to know that you were not too tired after our visit to Seville.'

'Thank you,' she answered. 'No, I woke up very fresh

74

this morning.'

'Courteous of you to drive over just to ask that simple question,' broke in Connall.

Averil's mood changed immediately. She turned towards Connall, intending to reprimand him for his own discourtesy, but Don Rodrigo forestalled her. 'I do not want to keep you from your own work, Señor Brunner. Averil and I have matters to discuss.'

Connall pulled himself up to his full height. 'Important matters, evidently, if you can interrupt your own and other people's siesta time. But actually, you're intruding. Averil and I were discussing the merits of learning to ride a donkey and then graduating to a horse. Will you permit me to finish our conversation?'

The icy irony was not lost on Don Rodrigo, who bowed to Averil, then walked the few steps to his car, entered it and slammed the door, but made no attempt to drive away.

Averil was now in an equivocal position. If she continued chatting to Connall, she would be treating Don Rodrigo with rudeness. If she dismissed Connall, who had been her lunch guest, in a summary fashion, that would be equally uncivil, but after a slight hesitation, she chose the latter course, convinced that Connall, being English, would not only understand her position, but be no worse for a taste of his own churlishness.

'Thank you, Connall, for your advice,' she now said sweetly. 'I'll consider what you say—about the donkey. Please excuse me.'

She walked towards Don Rodrigo's car. He leaned across and opened the door on the passenger side and as soon as she was seated, he drove off across the patio, through the wide opening where the gates were rarely closed, and was speeding along the road in the direction of his own villa.

'Please, not so fast, Don Rodrigo,' she pleaded, frightened that if another car were driven the opposite way at a similar speed, the result would be a disastrous head-on collision.

He slowed down to a more moderate pace. His face was still dark with anger.

'I would prefer it, Averil, if you did not encourage the

Englishman to call on you,' he said coldly.

'I can scarcely prevent him from calling at the villa.' Her answer was crisply spoken, for she did not intend that Don Rodrigo should take it upon himself to direct the comings and goings of her visitors.

'You can always refuse to see him,' he pointed out.

She remained silent at that, not anxious to argue with him in his present fiery mood. 'Where are we going?' she asked after a minute or two.

He shrugged. 'Anywhere, so that I can have you to myself without that man distracting you.'

'What was the matter you wanted to discuss with me?' she ventured after another silence.

Now he turned towards her and smiled. 'When I am with you, I forget what business I had in mind.'

'Then you'd better pay more attention to your driving now or else we shall run into a stone wall,' she warned him.

A few moments later he swung the car through a pair of imposing wrought iron gates and she realised that the long stone wall enclosed his home. Since she had visited the Villa Montelli only once before and then in the dark, she was now eager to see Don Rodrigo's house. At an arched entrance he stopped the car.

'It is possible to drive closer to our front door,' he explained as he helped her to alight, 'but I'd rather show you our villa and gardens if you will consent to walk.'

Fountains splashed softly into ornamental marble basins, banks of oleanders and geraniums in vivid colours were massed on either side of the central mosaic paved path and the trellised walls were wreathed with climbing plants.

'This is not really our patio, but only one of the outside gardens,' he told her.

He led her through the opening of a high carved wood door and the sight made Averil gasp with astonishment.

'Lovely!' she murmured softly, gazing at the series of arches that ran round the hollow square, every pillar entwined with festoons of greenery, the spaces above the arch joins decorated with sculptured heads.

'Those represent my ancestors,' Don Rodrigo explained.

76

'Perhaps they were not all as handsome as they appear there on the walls.'

A gallery with a stone balustrade ran round the upper floor, with handsome windows opening on to it, each embrasure decorated with carvings.

On the floor of the courtyard itself were beds of exotic flowers, interspersed with miniature orange or lemon trees, and Averil had to look closely to see that all were in concealed pots resting on the tiled floor.

Don Rodrigo conducted her around the entire length and breadth of the patio, allowing her to examine every picture on the walls, the brackets that held pottery or glass, the small items of dark wood furniture.

'It's an amazing place,' she said with enthusiasm. 'I had no idea when I came here that night that it was so beautiful.'

He smiled knowingly. 'Ah, but that was because I brought you into the house through a different way.'

Now he led her through further arches and corridors that opened out of the main building, until she confessed that she was hopelessly lost.

'I fear that my aunt, Doña Isabella, will still be taking her siesta and will not care to be disturbed, so perhaps I may show you the rest of our *cortijo*?'

All the time that he displayed to her admiring gaze the other courtyards with the stables, the horse boxes, the cottages where some of the staff lived, the shrubbery that was almost a maze, the idea grew in Averil's mind that he was exhibiting his wealth, his possessions, his status as a nobleman with ancient lineage and long-established roots in the district. 'Here is my kingdom,' she thought he was saying, and indeed, she was impressed, but what was his object?

She wondered if this had been his intention in driving to her villa this afternoon or if he had thought of it when he saw Connall and was now deliberately setting out to prove that Don Rodrigo de Montilla, with all his other family names incorporated, was a man of substance, whereas Connall was nothing but an employee of a road-making firm working for the Spanish government.

After a while he now indicated a stone bench in a tiny

77

alcove of shrubs, secluded from the rest of the gardens.

'If you will sit down, Averil, I'll tell you of my new plans,' he began. 'You know that next week is Holy Week and I'm sure you will want to see the various spectacles and processions in Seville, so I have arranged that you shall stay with Señora Rabell, whom you already know. Then with her friends and some of mine, we shall make up parties to go to the events. In that way you will be able to see many sides of the Spanish character and way of life. I shall drive you to Seville on Saturday, for Palm Sunday is the beginning of the festivities.'

Averil did not speak, for she was almost choking with indignation. If it had been Connall so calmly arranging schedules for her in this lordly fashion, she would have jumped up and shouted, 'How dare you order my life in your own neat and tidy way!' Bur she was faced with Don Rodrigo and she was anxious not to offend him. All the same, he must learn that she was not a puppet eager to respond when he pulled the strings.

'You do not approve?' Don Rodrigo asked with concern.

'No, it's not that.' She hesitated, trying to find words that would not insult him, yet leave her with an option to accept or decline. 'I'm not quite sure how long I shall be staying in Spain. You realise that I'm not just here on holiday. I have to watch what I spend when it's my great-aunt who is paying for it.' That was a fatal admission, for he pounced on the fact that she would be spared all expense.

'It will be our entire pleasure,' he said, 'to give you every kind of hospitality. Please do not worry about that.'

'Thank you,' she replied, feeling that events were moving too fast and the ground was slipping under her feet. 'Yet, all the same, I'd like time to consider your—your invitation. I have arrangements to make in the villa and many other things.'

He smiled at her, a slow, ardent smile that brushed aside mundane trifles. 'There is nothing that you need do. You know you are completely free.' He grasped her hand and drew her towards him. 'Come, Averil, it would give me such pleasure if you would permit me to escort you throughout the week.'

His words were not well chosen, for now she sensed that he was thinking more of displaying to his friends his new English acquaintance than of her delight in the exciting events that would take place in Seville.

She rose, rather more abruptly than she intended, and pulled her hand out of his clasp. 'It is kind of you to offer, but I can't decide now. I'll let you know—tomorrow.' She saw the cold expression creep over his face and was momentarily appalled by her own curtness. Yet she knew that if she added a few softer words, she would lose her whole argument. He would take her in his arms and persuade her that she had not meant what she said.

She walked slowly away from the alcove and he followed her. When they arrived near the stables a horse whinnied, no doubt at hearing footsteps close by, and Don Rodrigo said, 'If I had known you wanted a horse to ride, I could easily lend you one of mine.'

'I haven't learned to ride yet,' she replied shortly.

'Then I would be most happy to teach you.'

This time Averil turned towards him and laughed. 'I can't win, can I?'

But he did not understand the shade of meaning implied. 'I can say that you *have* won. You have won my heart completely.'

The household seemed to be arousing from the afternoon siesta and Don Rodrigo suggested that Averil might like to take coffee with his aunt, Doña Isabella.

'I'm not really dressed for afternoon occasions,' she objected. She was still wearing cream trousers and blue shirt in which she had set out for her morning walk before meeting Connall. 'Please give my apologies to Doña Isabella and perhaps I might be asked another time?'

'You are always welcome at any time,' he returned warmly. 'And now? You wish me to drive you back to your villa?'

'If it's no trouble.'

He gave her a comical look of hopeless resignation. 'When will you learn that I am never troubled by your demands? I am not like the Englishman who makes a trouble of everything.'

'Oh? Does he? In what way?' she asked as she accompanied Don Rodrigo towards the spot where he had left his car.

'Oh, I can't be bothered to talk about him,' he muttered.

When Averil arrived at the villa and Don Rodrigo had driven away, Gonzalo told her that the English *señor* had chosen a particular donkey for her to ride.

She grinned a little, remembering Connall's threat to select a difficult animal. 'Is he quiet?' she queried.

'Very quiet. *She* knows the way also and will not take you into danger.'

She glanced at Gonzalo and noticed the sincere concern on his face. In his voice, too, there was none of that surliness that he had adopted earlier soon after her arrival in Spain.

'Thank you, Gonzalo. I shall look forward to riding her. Has she a name?'

'Of course. All *burros* have names. She is called Que Pasa?'

'Que Pasa?' echoed Averil. 'But surely that only means "what is the matter?" '

Gonzalo grinned. 'We always give names like that in Spain to our animals. That one over there is called El Verano.'

'Summer,' murmured Averil. 'And is another called Winter?'

'No, *señorita*, but we have a horse called Venga Conmigo.'

She laughed at that. 'Come with me,' she translated. 'A definite invitation.'

'Will you ride tomorrow, *señorita*?' asked Gonzalo.

'Yes, in the morning.'

'I will have her ready,' he promised.

When she mounted, Gonzalo suggested that he would accompany her for at least part of the way.

'As you please,' she agreed, 'although I think I'm fairly safe on a quiet little donkey.'

'True, but you could also see some of the work being done on the vines and other places.'

'Yes, that would be interesting.' She set off with Gonzalo

on his chestnut horse and was aware that her feelings were mixed. On the one hand, she was pleased at what she considered a more co-operative attitude on Gonzalo's part, inviting her to take a real interest in the welfare of the estate. Yet it had been her intention, she now admitted to herself, to ride towards the track of the new road, in the opposite direction from the terraced vines. This was about the time when Connall was somewhere in the neighbourhood, but she quelled any idea of happy anticipation at meeting him on his rounds. Occasionally as she rode with Gonzalo, she gave a backward look over her shoulder across the grassy meadows to see if in the distance there was a sign of an approaching horseman, but there was none, and she was inordinately disappointed.

CHAPTER FIVE

WHEN Averil returned from her ride, leaving Gonzalo to finish his supervising of the men, she noticed a luxurious car standing there and wondered who the caller was. She quickly dismounted and led the donkey Que Pasa? to a stall, where a boy took charge of her.

Voices floated towards her from the covered part of the patio where there was usually a table and a few chairs for resting in the shade.

Connall came out of the shadow. 'Enjoyed your ride?' he asked, but before she could answer, he turned towards someone behind him. 'You have a visitor, Averil. Señorita Renata Bonaventa.'

The two girls greeted each other. 'I was coming home to Cadiz,' explained Renata, 'so I thought to break my journey here and see this estate to which I am entitled.'

'An excellent idea,' remarked Connall with enthusiasm.

Averil give him a a sharp glance. Where was its excellence, when she had been given no opportunity to prepare for Renata's surprise visit?

'I'm sorry I didn't know you were coming,' she said now to Renata.

'Oh, but it is good to see the place in its natural state without special preparations,' observed Renata.

'Quite right,' put in Connall. His hearty tone irritated Averil. Soon he would be pointing out all the faults and drawbacks of the Villa Serena and its surroundings.

'But you must come in,' she said politely to Renata. 'Wiil you stay to lunch?'

'I took the liberty of ordering some wine for Señorita Bonaventa,' said Connall smoothly. 'I had no idea how long you would be out and I was sure you would want me to do that.'

Now he was speaking as though he were the butler.

'I would like very much to lunch with you,' Renata said to Averil. Then she gave Connall a ravishing smile. 'You also are staying to lunch?'

Averil saw immediately that she was in a cleft stick. Without looking at him, she waited for Connall to declare that he had urgent business elsewhere, but he made no attempt to break the lengthy pause and when at last she gave him a swift glance, she saw the blandly hopeful expression on his face, like a dog sitting up to beg for a tasty morsel.

She gave him an icy smile. 'Naturally Connall stays to lunch here whenever he has the right opportunity.'

Marta had evidently been forewarned of the guest and took pains to serve an attractive meal of gazpacho followed by veal cutlets in a spicy sauce.

Even though the meal was protracted and afterwards the three sat outside in the patio with their coffee, Connall was evidently in no hurry to leave. When he finished one long thin cigar, he lit another.

'But of course you want to inspect some of the estate,' he said at last to Renata. 'The house is not so important. One can always live elsewhere.'

'My house in Cadiz is perhaps not luxurious,' she told him, 'but it is adequate.'

'Right, then. Shall we go?' Connall rose to escort Renata and again Averil's blood boiled at his proprietorial manner. As though *he* owned the place!

She placed herself now on the other side of Renata as together the trio strolled across the patio, glancing at the stables and outbuildings. Near the entrance to the road was a small piece of garden with half a dozen stone steps mounting to a bank of shrubbery.

'If you will please step up this way, Señorita Bonaventa,' suggested Connall, 'you could see some of the vineyards and melon rows.'

Renata unhesitatingly put her hand into Connall's while he helped her up to the bank. Averil, lagging behind, had to scramble up without Connall's gallant aid.

Renata seemed to find more interest in Connall's face than in the fields and vine terraces pointed out to her. 'Yes, it all seems very agreeable,' she said.

You should have been here a fortnight or so ago when it

was raining a downpour day after day, thought Averil resentfully.

Averil was first to descend the steps, then turned just in time to hear Renata's exclamation of dismay and see the way Connall caught her in his arms when she stumbled down the last step.

Oh, very prettily done, was Averil's contemptuous mental comment. Aloud, she said, 'You are not hurt, I hope?'

Renata smiled enchantingly first at Averil, then gave the full share to Connall. 'No, indeed. I am thankful to Señor Connall.'

So it was Christian names already. When they all returned to the villa, Averil escorted her guest through several of the downstairs rooms which had mercifully been tidied within the last day or two, and hoped that Renata would not notice the shabbiness too much.

It was late afternoon when Renata protested that she must leave and as Averil had guessed, Connall immediately offered to escort Señorita Bonaventa as far as the fork in the road where she would pick up the main route to Cadiz.

'That is most kind of you,' Renata replied, 'but you must have many important matters to attend to. But thank you for spending so much time with me.'

'Not in the least. It's been a pleasure,' he replied.

Yet Averil had the satisfaction of noting that he looked slightly disappointed. But when Renata entered her car, she consulted a road map, then leaned out to ask Connall to point out the right road.

'This one,' he answered. 'Look, I'd better come with you after all.'

Oh, how clever she was, this Spanish girl with the lovely face and luminous eyes! The gentle refusal first, followed by the determined beckoning.

'Connall can probably show you where his new road will cut the estate in half!' called Averil.

Renata lifted her gaze from the map. 'A new road?' Then she smiled with delight. 'Oh, that is good! I shall be very rich, for the government will pay for the road.'

With a wave of her hand Renata started the car and Averil watched as the girl with Connall beside her drove out into the road. She entered the villa and went up to her bedroom to stand staring out of the window, but seeing nothing of the view before her. Instead, she saw Renata lightly clasped in Connall's arms, Renata's beaming smile, Connall's captivated looks and honeyed words when he spoke to her.

Oh, well, what was the use of taking notice of Connall's varying moods? He had pointed out to Averil most emphatically that he was not the marrying kind of man, but he certainly fell over himself with attentions when a new girl appeared on the scene.

After a while Averil calmed her tangled emotions and settled herself in one of the downstairs rooms to examine some of the accounts that Gonzalo had brought to her last night. She was trying to comprehend the scribbled bits of paper, full of Spanish abbreviations and difficult to decipher, when the young girl Lola came in to announce that the English señor had called.

'Tell him I'm busy,' she snapped, but Connall was already entering the room before the maid could leave.

'Busy?' he echoed. 'Then I won't hinder you. I merely came to collect my horse from your patio.'

'I didn't know you'd left it behind.'

'I'm not the kind of man who lets his horse run behind a car,' he retorted. 'Where should I have put him? On top of Renata's car?'

She put down her pen and half turned to face him. 'I'm so glad you got on so well with Renata—especially at a first acquaintance. Or could I be wrong about that and you already knew her?'

He began to grin with delight. He pulled forward a chair and sat down only a couple of yards away from Averil.

'I know one or two of the ladies in Cadiz, but as it happens, not that one.'

'Then you made good use of the time while you were waiting for me to return.'

'And how could I know when you'd return from your first donkey ride?'

She saw it was hopeless to pierce his self-satisfaction in that way, so she tried another tack. 'I can't understand why

85

you were so anxious to enthuse about everything here. Do you want her claim to succeed and mine—or rather my great-aunt's—to fail?'

He drew a deep breath and now leaned his elbows on the table where she was working. 'Some questions that require thoughtful answers. Do I want her claim to succeed? Well, one point in her favour is that she's a relative of Don Francisco and she *is* Spanish.'

'And that gives her more right than——?'

'Your great-aunt Freda is an absentee landowner—that is, if she is legally entitled to this place. Absentee landlords are the curse of a country like this, where the owners ought to live on the farms or properties.'

'Don Francisco lived here all the time, apparently, yet the estate was neglected.'

'Probably only in his later years. In many cases, owners live in Madrid or Valencia or Cordoba and never even visit their estates once in a blue moon. Every year they expect their manager to hand over the profits to enable them to continue to live in comfort.'

Averil stared at him in surprise. 'I'd no idea that you felt so strongly against the idea of an English family taking it over. Is there anything wrong about us? I've always understood that in the past most of the sherry firms were English to start with, even if they married into Spanish families.'

'But your great-aunt Freda is in no position to do so. You've said yourself that she's an invalid and that's why you're here in her place.' He gave her a swift, piercing glance. 'Unless, of course, you have ideas about running the Serena estate yourself?'

Under his gaze she coloured. 'Of course not. You know that I'm here only to untangle the legal side.'

'Exactly,' he retorted in triumph. 'Then you'll return to England and let Gonzalo manage or mismanage, as the case may be.'

He had caught her again in a trap of words from which it was difficult to escape. At last she said quietly, 'Well, I still think you needn't have boosted up everything quite so much.'

'Don't be daft!' he said harshly. 'If I'd run it down and

told her how dilapidated everything was, she'd have soon known that there were reasons for not wanting her to bother with it. You were the one who told her about the new road.' He shot an accusing glance at Averil. 'You did that because you were trying to get even with me.'

'Why should I do that?' she demanded, colour flaming into her cheeks.

He rested his chin on his clasped knuckles. 'Because I think you're just the tiniest bit jealous.'

'Not in the least,' she replied offhandedly. 'No need for that.'

'No?'

'No,' she snapped. 'Your friendships with women are quite ephemeral, so you've told me——'

'No, no, I didn't say that. I've some very good women friends here in Spain whom I've known for a year or more.'

'Really? How faithful!'

'They happen to be married.'

She laughed hollowly. 'Then you're safe, of course. None of them expects you to marry her.'

'That's right. No one so far expects me to marry her.'

His direct look as he said those firm words sent her pulses leaping, but she forced herself to maintain her own unwavering gaze. His mouth was set in a hard line and there was none of his usual bantering look in his eyes. Eventually she turned her head away.

He stood up abruptly. 'Would you like to come to Cadiz with me tomorrow?'

His change of mood was disconcerting. 'To visit Renata?' she queried, seeking refuge in further mild provocation.

'Yes, among other things. She invited me to lunch, both of us, in fact.'

She caught that slight amendment to an invitation that had probably not included her. 'I'm sure she would rather you went without me,' she said smoothly.

He sighed with exasperation. 'Of all the silly little gooses——'

'Geese!' she broke in.

'*Gooses!*' he shouted. 'One day I really will shake you

87

and knock some sense into that silly head of yours.'

'A treat in store for me,' she replied.

'Dammit, will you come or not?'

She had also risen from her chair and glared at him. 'I have a prior engagement,' she said slowly and with emphasis.

'With the handsome Don, of course.'

'Of course. He has invited me to Seville for all next week. I shall be leaving tomorrow.'

He took a deep breath, held it for what seemed a long time, then let it out in an explosive attack. 'You prize idiot! He'll cart you around during Holy Week, show you the processions, the festivities, the fireworks, and by the time you come back here, you'll have signed away the Serena estate to him.'

'How could I when——' she began, but he was already halfway out of the room.

'Go to Seville and enjoy yourself!' was his parting command, and to Averil it sounded a menacing farewell as though he had told her to go to hell and stay there.

When he had gone she stood in the room for some moments, shaken by the angry scene, aware that she had probably behaved childishly and furious that in her temper, she had committed herself to accepting Don Rodrigo's plan for a week in Seville. What had possessed her to tell Connall of that arrangement? He would have known in due course, but she need not have flung it in his teeth in that way.

She slumped into a chair. Now she began to examine her own motives. Had she really wanted to go to Seville with Don Rodrigo right from the moment he asked her? Had it needed the catalyst of a rival invitation from Connall to make her decision for her? She could not decide at this moment, for her thoughts were too jumbled for clear conclusions, but deep down in her heart, she realised that his taunt about jealousy had struck home. This afternoon when Renata had practised the coquette on Connall, Averil had been filled with appalling spasms of plain and simple jealousy.

Now she brushed the thoughts aside. Nobody was ever jealous unless they had a deep longing for the person con-

cerned and she was certainly not longing for a deeper regard from Connall.

Somehow she had to contrive to extricate herself from
the plan to go to Seville and realised with a sharp sense of
bitterness that if Connall had asked her to go later in the
week to see some of the processions, she would gladly have
gone. So where did this leave her? She shelved her present
problems and tried again to concentrate on the accounts and
bills, but these, too, she had to put aside, for between her
and the account book she could see only Connall's anger-
contorted face as he marched out of the room.

Just before dinner, Gonzalo's daughter Vanna brought a
letter for Averil.

'Thank you, Vanna.'

'Señor Don Rodrigo said I was to wait for an answer,'
said the girl.

Averil guessed already what was in the note, and the few
lines scribbled on heavy crested notepaper confirmed her
ideas. Naturally he needed to know her decision about Seville.

'Will you wait a few minutes, Vanna?' she asked. 'I'll
write an answer.'

Averil went up to her own room, trying to gain time
before she had to make up her mind. She thought wildly at
first of telling Don Rodrigo that she was going to Cadiz
tomorrow to see Renata, but he would immediately offer to
take her and the whole affair would look silly if she and
Don Rodrigo arrived in Cadiz in one car with Connall in
another.

In the end she pleaded that she had many arrangements
to make in the villa and with Gonzalo on the estate to get
the place in a flourishing condition during the short summer. This at least had the merit of being true. At the end of
her note she hinted at a vague promise later on to attend
some festivity with him.

Downstairs in the hall she gave the note to Vanna. Then
it occurred to her that the girl had already walked from the
Montilla villa and would be forced to walk back in the
dark.

'Vanna, have you to walk to Don Rodrigo's?'

The girl grinned. 'No, *señorita*. Manuel brought me on his motor-cycle and will take me back.'

'Oh, good.' Averil knew that Manuel was Don Rodrigo's foreman on the Montilla estate.

At dinner, Averil had little appetite and soon afterwards she crept to the seclusion of her room, read for a while, then went to bed. But sleep would not come, for she was gnawed by doubts and anxieties that had not worried her after Don Rodrigo's ardent attentions in Seville and on the way home. It was strange that she should be so upset by Connall's iron-hearted rancour, when all she wanted was his friendship, an English helping hand in a life that was foreign to her in every sense. She wanted desperately to retain that friendship, resolutely refusing to recognise that she desired or needed anything more than that. Yet when he needled her, she could not resist acrid retorts. Now she had wilfully deprived herself of a visit to Cadiz. Even if at Renata's house, he gave all his attention to her, Averil would still have relished his company on the journey and return.

When she rose next morning, most of her problems still unsolved, Averil decided that a ride on the donkey Que Pasa? might soothe her. She waited while a young boy saddled the donkey and then she rode off, carefully avoiding any direction in which she might be met by a car containing Connall.

No doubt he was already on his way to Cadiz, anxious to spend as much time with Renata as possible. It occurred to Averil that if Renata was the daughter of Don Francisco's sister, surely it was odd that she had apparently never visited the Villa Serena on some previous occasion. Cadiz was comparatively near, certainly not a distance that would prevent a sister visiting her brother or keep a niece from her uncle. Some sort of quarrel or estrangement? If that were the case, apparently Renata had no scruples about claiming the Serena estate.

When Averil returned to the villa, she half expected to find Don Rodrigo there, angrily asking her why she had refused to go to Seville with him. To her relief, there were no visitors. She spent the rest of the day writing letters to her parents and her great-aunt Freda, but to the latter she made no mention of Renata as a rival claimant. That matter could wait until there was more likelihood that the Spanish girl might succeed.

The next morning, Palm Sunday, Averil discovered a large, ornate palm cross affixed to the front door of the villa and asked Marta who had made it.

'My daughter, Vanna,' said the woman proudly. 'She is very clever with her fingers.'

'I heard that Manuel, Don Rodrigo's foreman, came with Vanna the night before last when she brought a message to me.'

'Manuel would like to marry Vanna, but she is looking higher than to be the wife of a foreman on the estate. There is always work, work, work.' Marta wiped her hands on her apron. 'Don Rodrigo has promised to take Vanna to his house in Madrid. There she would meet many people, perhaps someone rich. Here, in these parts, there is no one to meet.'

'I suppose Don Rodrigo does very little entertaining when he is here at the Montilla villa?' asked Averil.

Marta shook her head. 'Not much. He and his aunt, Doña Isabella, sit looking at each other.' Then she gave Averil a swift upward glance. 'But now you are here, he likes to take you to Seville and to his villa. Perhaps soon he will give a dance for you.'

Averil laughed. 'I doubt that very much. In any case, I may be here for only a month or two. Then I shall have to return to England.'

Marta's face showed dismay. 'You go back and not come here again?'

'Oh, no. It is possible that I shall come back, but I have to talk with my great-aunt and tell her all I can about the estate.'

Marta moved towards the stove to stir soup in a large pot. 'It is sad, also for Gonzalo it is sad. We are here and have to manage as best we can, and the owner does not care about us or what we do, whether we are happy or not.'

'But Don Francisco lived here all the time,' protested Averil.

Marta shrugged. 'He lived with his books and his papers.

He wrote many hours. If Gonzalo went in to ask him for advice, Don Francisco said, "Go away, leave me in peace. Do as you think best." '

After a slight pause, Averil asked quietly, 'Would you like to have the owner here permanently, ordering you about?'

'Yes,' replied Marta with emphasis. 'But not a woman. Such places need a man. Oh, you are kind, *señorita*, and you would do your best, but not the same as a man!'

Averil reflected that if Renata's claim succeeded, that would still mean a woman in charge of the Serena estate.

'But there is no man to inherit. Don Francisco had no son,' she pointed out.

'There is Don Rodrigo. Perhaps one day he will take it.'

Averil had no wish to pursue this particular line of hazard. If Marta meant that Averil's marriage to Don Rodrigo would ensure a joint estate, then that was quite out of the question, and not only the marriage part. Great-aunt Freda had other nephews and nieces besides Averil and her sister Dinah.

During the rest of the day Averil mulled over some of Marta's remarks. She could understand how unsatisfactory the situation was when Gonzalo and Marta had to manage in the owner's absence, or even when as in the case of Don Francisco, the owner refused to be bothered with management. Connall's words echoed in her mind—'absentee landlords are the curse of a country like this . . .' but it was easy for Connall to lay down the law. He was free to roam about, ploughing his roads across other people's land, free to travel from one country to another.

In the late afternoon she went out for a walk. Grass now covered the large areas of swamp and horses and cattle had been let in to forage in the meadows. In some places, the animals stood in water up to their knees; Connall had warned her that much of the underlying water would remain until the middle of June. Enormous flocks of terns and coots were collecting grasses to build their nests. Averil wondered how secure such nests could be, but here again, Connall had told her that the birds built large round flat constructions that floated on the water.

She became impatient with herself for allowing her mind to dwell on Connall, even though the little bits of information he gave her from time to time were enlightening. He had promised to show her what he called the 'egg-harvest' when men came in boats to collect the eggs for the sale in the towns. She doubted whether he would bother about such promises now that angry scenes had come between them. Besides, she thought with a smile, he had a new attraction in Renata.

She paused, deciding that perhaps she had walked far enough, for she had to return along the same fairly hard path the way she had come. The sun had set and now for the first time she saw the beautiful mauve light that spread across the swamplands. 'Amethyst', Connall had called it, and that was a true description. The colour crept like a faint mist, veiling the sharp greens of the meadows so that in the distance they looked like tulle caught in warm moonlight.

Averil caught her breath with wonder at the sight of this lovely glow. No, not a glow, a suffusing radiance, and in the same instant she became aware of the hold this countryside had taken of her. She understood why Connall loved it and she would be sorry to leave when she had to return to England.

Several times on her way back to the villa, she turned to look behind her, but the amethyst hues had gone.

A couple of days later Averil learned that Don Rodrigo had gone off to Madrid to spend a few days with other members of his family.

Vanna, Marta's daughter, brought the news and was evidently taking the opportunity of enjoying some extra time in her own home while the master was away.

Averil saw the girl sitting in the patio with her father during the late afternoon.

'He is very angry about something,' Vanna informed Averil, with enthusiasm.

'Who?' queried Averil, pretending innocence.

'Don Rodrigo! He spoke much with Doña Isabella and

93

when he said he would go to Madrid, she said it might do his bad temper good. She would be glad to be without him for a week or two, she said. And the maid who served his breakfast——'

'Thank you, Vanna,' broke in Averil, uneasy at this narrative of servants' gossip. 'Perhaps Don Rodrigo has business worries and needs a change in Madrid.'

The look that Vanna slanted at Averil conveyed a world of innuendo. Averil was aware of an uncomfortable notion that one way or another, very little took place in either the Montilla household or the Serena villa that was not known and chatted over by their respective staffs, with Vanna as the connecting link.

How much Vanna acted as general informant Averil did not realise until she saw Connall the next day when he called to tell Gonzalo that a small stretch of the new road under construction would be blocked for the next two or three days. Averil saw him as she rode into the patio on her favourite little donkey. She dismounted and spoke caressingly to Que Pasa?, hoping that Connall would leave without speaking, but when out of the corner of her eye she saw him mount his horse and wheel towards the gate, she was filled with indignation mixed with regret.

She led the donkey into the stall and was startled when Connall's voice behind her barked, 'What was Seville like?'

She had to blink back the tears before she could turn to face him. 'And what was Cadiz like?'

An expression of beatific enjoyment spread across his face. 'Fine. Fine indeed. I was well received at Señorita Bonaventa's house, and that's no lie, for I did actually go. Why didn't you go to Seville?'

'I can change my mind, can't I?' she protested. 'How do you know that I didn't go and come back again?'

Now he grinned and swung himself off his horse to stand beside her. 'Because my private spy told me that you didn't go at all.'

'Vanna, of course. She's everyone's spy,' mumbled Averil.

'Don't dare to run that girl down,' he warned her. 'Vanna is one of the most useful creatures around here.'

'Naturally, if you're interested in prying into other people's concerns——'

'And now he's gone off to Madrid and probably never even asked you to accompany him,' murmured Connall teasingly.

'There was no reason why he should.'

'There might be every reason why he should not!' he snapped. 'Escorting you around Seville to show an English visitor the sights and sounds of Holy Week is one thing. But hasn't it entered your empty little head that in Madrid he'll be among most of the Montilla clan, and the subject of dear Rodrigo's marriage is quite a talking point? No doubt they have a selection of their friends' daughters and their daughters' friends for him to run his eye over yet again.'

'And why should that worry me?' she queried, some of her confidence regained.

'Averil, my sweet, you can't fool me. Admit that you're flattered and pleased that the handsome Don has cast admiring eyes upon you.'

'I'm also aware that a little flattery and admiration is all that's meant.'

'Then keep it that way.' He tapped her on the shoulder. 'The man's a menace with his good looks and his purring Spanish compliments.'

'Thanks for the warning,' she said lightly. 'If I didn't know that you weren't the marrying kind of man, I'd be inclined to believe that you were—just the tiniest bit—jealous, shall we say?'

The teasing expression left his face instantly, to be replaced by a scowl which almost frightened her. The seconds went by before he spoke. 'Fortunately, jealousy is an emotion I can't afford.' Then it seemed that the black mood lifted as suddenly as it had descended. 'It occurred to me as I was leaving your villa that as you're probably at a loose end, you might like to come with me to Seville on Good Friday?'

His invitation was so unexpected that she took refuge in laughter, while she scrabbled in her mind for a suitable reply.

'Why don't you take the beautiful Renata?' she asked.

95

'Because she's busy in Cadiz entertaining some of her relatives.'

'I'm proud to be second best.' She was thrilled to be asked to go almost anywhere with him, but she was not going to yield too suddenly.

'For all you know you might be fourth—or fifth—best. I have a small but select circle of feminine acquaintances.'

She looked up to meet his eyes, but he was now standing with his back to the light and she could not see what expression his eyes held. 'Come on, girl, don't shilly-shally, or I shall go to Seville on my own and snatch a *señorita* riding behind her *caballero*.'

'That would be fun to watch you do that. All right, I'll let you know about Friday.'

'You'll let me know now, this minute.' He seized her shoulders and gave her a rather ungentle shake. She ought to have been indignant at being treated like a child, but she revelled in it, aware that it would be very heaven if he folded her in his arms and kissed her with an intensity alarming and desirable at the same time.

She waited, her face only inches from his own, but he released her and moved towards his horse.

'Yes, I'll come,' she said in a small voice, ashamed and humbled at her own capitulation, as well as that tense moment when he must have known she was hoping to be kissed.

'Just in time! Be ready at seven. I shall have to make an early start.'

He had mounted and clattered away before she could even frame an answer. As she stood there she wondered what Don Rodrigo would think when he learned that having refused to accompany him to Seville, she accepted Connall's offer. Yet she could not quell this light-hearted, almost light-headed, feeling of joy that enveloped her. In spite of their mutual antagonism, he was still interested enough to take her to Seville. Her heart was leaping about like a mad thing as she went indoors and up to her bedroom, where she pulled open the door of the wardrobe and wondered what she would wear on Friday.

CHAPTER SIX

THE main approaches to Seville were crammed with vehicles, cars, lorries, vans, mule-drawn carts, all streaming in the direction of the centre of the city.

'Not a good time to come in,' muttered Connall to Averil, as he tried to find short cuts through side streets. 'Don Rodrigo had more sense when he asked you to stay here for the whole week.'

Averil merely smiled, but said nothing. She was more delighted to be in the company of Connall for a single day than touring around with Don Rodrigo for a week.

Connall had to leave the car in a small square a little way from the Cathedral. 'We shall have to walk the rest. We'll go towards the Sierpes, but whether we shall get in there, I don't know.'

'Yes, I know the Sierpes, the narrow street that means "serpents",' she said.

But Connall changed his mind. 'No, we'll go there later. We'll try the waterfront first and see a procession setting out.'

He knew the streets of the city very well, but it took some time before eventually he and Averil emerged by the river close to the Golden Tower. He took her to a riverside warehouse where twenty or thirty stevedores were preparing to carry one of the floats.

'When you see the huge floats apparently being airborne along the streets,' Connall told her, 'you don't always realise the sweat and strain of the men who carry the Virgin.'

The men, dressed in their own trousers and shirts, often shabby, with rope sandals, began to adjust each other's canvas bags filled with sawdust and sand. Each man placed the bag about the size of a large cushion on top of his head so that the sand fell towards the end of the bag over his shoulders.

'The bag takes the weight to some extent,' explained

97

Connall, who was greeted from time to time by one or other of the men.

When the men were ready, Connall and Averil followed them to the church where the confraternity waited with the float of the Virgin.

'There are probably forty or fifty of these confraternities, brotherhoods, that is, all over the city,' Connall explained. 'Each has its own procession and the members meet all through the year to provide funds for their own particular church and perhaps give something to the poor people of the district.'

Averil watched while one man from the confraternity paid each of the float bearers his hundred pesetas. Then they crawled under the float, built on a large wooden stand, with a handsomely-dressed and bejewelled Virgin on top. With the brocaded skirts of the float adjusted to hide the bearers, they waited for the captain to give the signal. Then as one man, they rose to a standing position and the beautiful Virgin seemed to float upwards of her own accord. When they took the first step forward, the crowds in the street, on the balconies and at the upper windows of houses, broke into ecstatic cries.

In front of the float marched the hooded members of the confraternity, only their eyes occasionally gleaming through the slits in their tall stiffened hoods; each man carried a long taper held at an angle from the hips.

'Do all the floats go out around the same time?' asked Averil.

'No. Some leave at midnight and march all night, others go out at dawn or eight or nine o'clock and wander through the streets during the day, but most of them actually march for about twelve hours.'

'It must be very tiring for the bearers,' Averil observed.

'And the hooded penitents,' he added. 'Some of them walk barefoot with chains around their ankles. It's a penance men set themselves.'

'I don't think I realised how much religious significance all these processions had in Spain. I thought it was a little bit solemn, but the rest of it was carnival.'

'Carnival comes later, along with the horse fair.'

She wanted to ask Connall when the fair took place, but that would seem like begging him to take her to the fair.

When the whole of the procession had passed and the crowds began to mill back and forth in the roadway until another float might arrive from another part of the city, Connall took Averil's arm and pulled her out of the throng.

'Somewhere we must eat,' he said, 'and most of the restaurants will be closed today, but I know a place.'

Averil was confident that he was very familiar with the city and knowledgeable about what was on offer.

After some pushing and struggling along a narrow street, she and Connall emerged into a wide avenue.

'Oh, there's the tobacco factory from *Carmen*,' she said, recognising the long building opposite the barracks.

'Did Rodrigo point it out to you?' he asked. 'I'm surprised that he'd show you anything so mundane.'

'That factory isn't mundane at all if it found a place in opera,' she countered.

But he was only laughing as he guided her towards a stall selling *churros*, those popular fritters cooked and eaten piping hot everywhere in Spain. There were also small plates of *tapas*, hors d'oeuvres containing shrimps, morsels of razor-fish, scraps of ham.

'Will you eat with me in this rough homespun fashion?' he queried, his eyes dancing with challenge.

'Of course. I'm hungry and I'll be delighted.'

'Not, of course, the elegant menu that Don Rodrigo would offer you,' he said.

'But Don Rodrigo isn't here to offer it,' she shot back, but that was a mistake.

'Do you wish he were?'

'You've lost your place in the queue,' she pointed out, as others crowded in front of Connall.

He still hung back, amused. 'I might take that answer in two ways. If you mean that I'm far behind Don Rodrigo in your particular queue——'

'No, I was talking about the strictly practical. If the man sells out of food before he's able to serve you, I shall die of hunger.'

Lazily, he turned away and approached the stall counter.

In only a few moments he was back with platefuls of food. Near the stall were a few benches and wooden tables and here Averil and Connall ate their outdoor picnic. She would have been just as pleased to share bread and cheese with him anywhere, for if ever she came again to Seville with Don Rodrigo and he took her to a smart restaurant, she would remember this simple meal eaten with Connall among a crowd of laughing and chattering Spaniards.

When they left the stall, he guided her through a maze of back streets where sometimes they had to wait for a procession to pass along a crossroad and then they were near the Cathedral with its beautiful Moorish tower, La Giralda, meaning the weathervane, with the figure of faith on top.

'Would you like to sit for a while in the Court of the Orange Trees?' Connall asked. 'Today it may be less crowded because most of the people are in the streets.'

Averil had only once previously glanced at this walled-in garden with the cathedral cloisters at one end. Long rows of orange trees perfumed the air and, as Connall had foreseen, only a few people occupied the benches, mostly young couples glad of a chance to sit in an oasis of quiet among the excited noise of bands and processions.

Now as she sat close to him, her earlier jaunty spirits deserted her, for she was filled with both a sense of elation and a dread of displaying undue emotion. If she had imagined that he would follow the example of other couples and hold her hand or pass an arm around her shoulders, she was quite mistaken, for he sat hunched forward, his hands loosely clasped between his knees.

Yet if he had given her no more than a lighthearted kiss in this public place, she would have been even more disappointed, for he had already made it quite clear that he was not the kind of man to fall in love at all, and probably less likely to fall in love with Averil. So any sign of affection would have been completely false and what could be more grieving than a kiss so lightly bestowed?

'How long do you expect to stay here in Spain?'

His sudden question startled her out of her thoughts.

'I'm not sure,' she answered. 'It depends on the lawyers, I suppose.'

100

What was now at the back of his mind? Was he trying to find out how much longer he would have to endure her presence at the Villa Serena or would her departure be a matter of regret to him?

'No use depending on lawyers. They won't fix matters in a hurry.'

'No, I suppose not, especially now that someone else has put in a claim.' Averil regretted that she had mentioned this matter, for an instant vision of Renata's beautiful face rose in front of her, followed by a flashback of that incident when Renata had pretended to stumble down the steps in the villa garden and been caught so expertly in Connall's arms.

When he now remained silent, she continued, 'I wouldn't be able to stay here very much longer in any case. My great-aunt Freda is not wealthy and it's been wonderful that she has paid all my expenses. I couldn't impose on her for an indefinite period in the hope that all the legal matters would be settled.'

'Then what? You'd go back to England?'

She tried to recover a little of her lost gaiety. 'That sounds as though you're hopeful of waving me farewell.'

He turned his face towards her and his expression was almost daunting in its severity. 'I was merely asking about your plans,' he snapped.

Her levity was extinguished in an instant. 'Yes, I'd be going back to England, but just when I'm not sure. Maybe another two or three weeks, probably not more.'

As he did not reply, she paused before asking, 'And you will leave when the new road is finished?' Surely she was entitled to ask him that in return for his own pointed inquiries.

'Long before then. My job is to supervise the foundations and see that it won't sink into a switchback after a week's rain. Another gang comes along to put on the finishing surfaces.'

So he would not be staying near Serena for much longer, she supposed. Her spirits plummeted to a nadir out of all proportion to his words. Oh, why did he have to tell her this depressing news today when she had come to spend an enjoyable day's sightseeing in his company?

But later in the afternoon when he had guided her towards the Sierpes, he seemed to have recovered some of his usual buoyancy. 'If we cut across this street, we shall be about halfway along the Sierpes and you'll see the floats at close quarters, so close that they're quite likely to give you a black eye if you're careless and don't watch out.'

A small bar on the corner of the side street had already closed in honour of the procession, for this was the most intense part of this parade.

Only a comparatively thin line of spectators could wedge themselves along the narrow street and Averil soon understood the reason. Connall spoke to a couple of young Spanish boys and with smiles and polite bows, they yielded their places to Connall and Averil, who squeezed themselves into the scanty space.

For the first few moments Averil could scarcely breathe. She felt heady with the rapture of being pushed against Connall in so intimate a position, but she fought down this stifling emotion and tried to focus her thoughts on the coming procession.

'Now you see what I mean,' whispered Connall as the first float appeared, a tableau of Jesus, and only just avoided scraping the projecting walls where the Sierpes was at its narrowest.

From beneath the enveloping brocade curtains around the base of the float, Averil could hear the grunts and whispers of the bearers as they manipulated their burden so that no damage could occur.

She turned towards Connall to whisper something about this exciting spectacle, but found that his gaze was upon her face and not on the tableau. For a split second she fancied that she glimpsed the warm light of admiration in his eyes, but instantly he jerked his head away to look across the street and she could not be sure whether her imagination was merely supplying wishful thinking. Yet with her body so close to his, she felt that he must be aware of her attraction to him, and she drew slightly away, but someone in the crowd jostled and pushed and again she was swung almost violently against Connall. This time he steadied her with his arm around her waist, but he did not look at her. His glance seemed stonily occupied with the moving pageant passing in front.

The second tableau with the Virgin came in sight, a magnificent figure in embroidered robes, crowned with a diadem and wearing a great wealth of jewellery and precious stones. A canopy of embroidered velvet surmounted the Virgin and silver vases of white carnations decorated the base of her float, lit by dozens of tall candles. In the dusk of twilight, this was a scene to remember, thought Averil.

At last the tension was relaxed as the floats moved towards the square at the exit of the Sierpes and on towards the Cathedral where the floats would be blessed.

Averil, too, experienced the immense relief that swept away the keyed-up sensation of the last half hour. She and Connall did not speak until they had joined the slowly drifting crowd along the street.

'Thank you, Connall,' she began sincerely. 'I was glad to be here today to see that beautiful sight.'

He took her wrist to guide her among the mass of people and her pulses leapt at his touch. 'Glad you liked it,' he said brusquely, as though he had taken her to an amusing play or a sports event.

She was chilled by his coolness, yet when an hour later he took her to a small restaurant he seemed to shed this icy manner.

The restaurant proprietor apologised for the fact that he had little to offer already cooked. 'The processions, you understand. We have been closed for half the day.'

'Naturally,' agreed Connall cheerfully. 'Then you can bring us Spanish omelettes and some cheese and a bottle of wine and we shall be happy.'

Averil almost blinked at this abrupt change of attitude, but told herself that these frequent switches of mood were all part and parcel of Connall's make-up, and she would have to accustom herself to them.

Her thoughts broke off with a suddenness that shocked

103

her. Accustom herself to what? Surely her mind was running far ahead of actual facts. For how long did she believe that Connall would play any permanent part in her life? A few more weeks at most, perhaps not as much. Then she would return to England and he would be off to some other part of Spain to survey and churn up another tract of land for a road.

'Come, Averil, pay attention.'

'Yes, I'm sorry. You were saying?'

'I was at that moment mercifully silent, but you were dreaming.' He gave her a piercing glance across the table, a glance that impelled all her guilty feelings to the surface and caused the colour to flush her cheeks.

'Yes, perhaps I was,' she admitted in a quiet voice, hoping he would not pursue the subject.

'Let me guess the lucky man who occupied your thoughts for so long. Not, I sincerely hope, Don Rodrigo?'

She shook her head and began to eat the omelette which had just arrived.

'I've suspected for some time that there's someone at home in England,' he continued.

'Suspect away!' His prolonged teasing discomfited her. 'You could be right.' Let him think that she was devoted to a man in her home town rather than let him hit on the real object.

Now, as she glanced swiftly upwards, she saw him nod, apparently with satisfaction. 'Quite right, too. I wouldn't like to think there was no one who would welcome you home again.'

'I have my family, too,' she reminded him. 'I'm not an orphan, nor bereft of friends.'

He sighed heavily. 'That's my trouble. I have no friends, no one to care a row of pins about me. Working from place to place, I never have the chance to make lasting friendships.'

'Perhaps the fault is yours,' she accused, taking the attack into his camp. 'Maybe you don't attract lasting friendships—except possibly among the girls you know. Or do you count those only among the casuals?'

He grimaced. 'I should have known not to expect any

kind of sympathy from you.' Then he changed the subject abruptly and spoke of some of his past road construction activities.

Averil was wholly glad of this new trend, directed away from herself, and by the time the bottle of wine was finished the time had flown by.

'When we go out again into the streets,' he told her as they left the restaurant, 'listen to the clapping.'

'Applause, do you mean?'

'Not exactly, but you must listen.'

Averil walked along with Connall for some distance before she understood. A woman passing in the dark was clapping her hands quite softly, but rhythmically as though she were chanting a silent song. Then a group behind her joined in with exactly the same rhythm. Averil listened and watched while the group straggled towards a more brilliantly-lit street and the sound of this soft clapping died away, but almost immediately another small group emerged from a side street and began to tap, but with a different rhythm interrupted occasionally by one staccato clap.

Averil leaned to Connall for enlightenment. 'Do people always do this at night?' she asked.

'No, only during this week. It becomes a kind of tattoo for spring in Seville.'

It was very late when Connall at last discovered his car, for the square where he had parked it was blocked by yet another procession on its way to the Cathedral. 'I expect the Civil Guard removed it,' he grunted, when he found it.

Averil was sleepy at first with the excitements and emotional fervour of the long day, but halfway along the road towards home, she became wide awake. Traffic on the road was heavy with returning travellers and she did not want to distract Connall's attention, but when he slowed down and curved towards a restaurant at the fork of a road, she was very much on the alert.

This was the place where Don Rodrigo had stopped when he brought Averil back from Seville after the visit to the notary and the stay at Señora Rabell's.

'Would you care for a drink?' asked Connall with deceptive politeness.

'Not really, but don't let me stop you.'

'One can't drink alone,' he objected, then added in that soft teasing voice he sometimes adopted, 'Not even Oloroso. In fact, particularly not Oloroso.'

'Oh, you've dragged up that old joke again,' she sighed. 'There's no other hostelry this side of Cadiz where I could take a lady. Well?'

'Oh, all right,' she assented, and slid out of the car. Secretly she could not resist that pleading in his voice. 'But if drinking Oloroso means what you say it does, I'd better be careful.'

'Oh, you must certainly take care,' he returned, as he joined her from his side of the car and took her arm across the stone courtyard. 'Bad enough to have amorous Spaniards making a nuisance of themselves, let alone English vagabonds who roam the roads of Spain and ought to know better, especially with one of their own nationality.'

The inn was full of people eating and drinking, laughing and chattering, with waiters and girls hurrying to and fro with trays of food and jugs and bottles of wine.

Connall found a table for two in a corner just vacated by two laughing Spaniards who declared to anyone who would listen that they were matadors and exhibiting their skill at the bullring on Sunday week.

'Are they matadors?' Averil asked.

'Probably not. Almost every young man dreams and hopes of showing off in the ring, but few ever manage it.'

The wine came and Averil found to her surprise that he had ordered Amontillado instead of the threatened Oloroso.

'Civilised and innocuous,' he said smugly, as he raised his glass to her.

'Are you referring to the wine or yourself?' she queried.

'Both!'

She laughed. In her mind she classed him as neither, for his profession entailed a rough life sometimes in uncomfortable circumstances. As to being innocuous, the very thought made her giggle inwardly. He was the most dangerous man she had so far met, for he stirred her wildest impulses, made havoc of her strongest resolutions. He treated her as an English girl casually met on one of his work sites, a companion to take to the procession or the fair, and with this she knew she must be content, but she longed constantly for something more than this, even though that longing was entirely in vain.

When he resumed the journey and finally deposited her in the patio of the Villa Serena, he put an arm around her shoulder and drew her towards him as they still sat in the car.

She imagined that her rapidly beating heart would betray her, but he asked, 'Enjoyed yourself?'

'Very much. Thank you for taking me.'

'Good.' He gave her a peck on her cheek somewhere near her left ear, then almost thrust her from him and scrambled out of the door his side.

'We must go to Seville again some time,' he said. 'Maybe the horse fair.'

'Maybe,' she rejoined.

As she climbed the stairs to her bedroom, she thought how coolly casual his invitations could sound. Connall resembled in some ways those offhand young men one met sometimes at dances—'we must come here again ... I'll give you a ring...' If you had a passing interest in them, they never telephoned; only the boring or clumsy or pompous kind rang when they could find no other partner at short notice.

Undoubtedly Connall was practised in the art of fending off unwelcome attentions from girls. At strategic moments he seemed to pull down a shutter, sealing himself off. Averil sighed. There was nothing she could do about changing his attitude. Then the thought of Renata entered like a needle. Was he more vulnerable to that fine Spanish beauty?

On the Monday after Easter, Don Rodrigo appeared at the Serena door. He was in riding clothes and accompanied by two horses, one on a leading rein.

'You must progress from a donkey to a horse,' he greeted Averil. 'I have come to give you a riding lesson. I promised that I would teach you.'

107

She glanced dubiously at the chestnut mare he indicated, hoping that the creature was not too spirited.

'But I'm not dressed for riding,' she demurred.

'You look entirely charming and suitably dressed as you are now,' he contradicted smoothly.

She was wearing brown trousers with a cream shirt. She was faintly irritated by his arrogant attitude in assuming that she would drop all her plans for the morning and consent to ride with him straight away. Yet, as he helped her to mount the mare and settle herself in the saddle, she knew that if Connall had done exactly the same this morning, she would have jumped at the chance.

In any case, she could not allow herself to lose face in front of Marta, and the maids giggling in the background.

The mare was smaller than Don Rodrigo's magnificent black and Averil realised that her mount was not much higher or wider than the donkey Que Pasa?

'You will be quite safe,' Don Rodrigo assured Averil as the two horses soberly walked out of the patio on to the road.

To her surprise and delight, Averil found after the first mile that she enjoyed being perched on the mare's back and viewing the countryside from a different height. 'I always feel that I'm too heavy for a donkey, although poor little animals, they have to carry more weighty burdens than me.'

Don Rodrigo turned off the road and took a path across what had been marshes only perhaps a fortnight ago and was now dry ground with only a few wet places.

Away to the west immense flocks of birds congregated on the grassy patches of land, terns and avocets chose the remaining lakes and sometimes nearer at hand there were hoopoes with their inquisitive long bills.

Averil allowed her attention to wander from guiding her horse and Don Rodrigo reminded her that although the mare knew all the roads and paths, it was still the rider's duty to attend to direction.

'I was watching the birds,' she admitted humbly.

'I must be forgiven if I spend most of my time watching you,' he returned in his accustomed gallant manner.

After a time he dismounted, then lifted her off the mare,

seizing the chance, of course, of hugging Averil around the waist.

While the two horses grazed by the side of the path, Don Rodrigo took Averil's hand.

'It was very naughty to send me to Madrid so that you could spend a day with the Englishman,' he accused her.

'I had no part in sending you to Madrid,' she protested.

'You refused to let me take you to Seville for a week, and then agreed to go with him.'

'Yes, but that was only for a day.'

'Then you mean that if I had offered only one day, you would have accompanied me?'

She laughed. 'You twist my words. Connall's invitation was only a casual one.'

'Why didn't he take Renata Bonaventa? He visited her house in Cadiz.'

Averil glanced at Rodrigo. 'You know everything that goes on, who goes where and with whom. Have you also your own private spy?'

She knew, of course, that Vanna had retailed all the news back and forth between the two houses. Really, that girl worked hard at keeping people informed.

'It is not spying, I assure you,' he said coldly. 'Naturally, I am eager to know what my rivals are doing in my absence.'

'You don't really think that Connall is a rival, do you?'

The words were heedlessly said, as she discovered the next moment, for he pulled her towards him and studied her face. 'Do you really mean that I have no rival? That you do love me and will marry me?'

She pulled away from him, but he tightened his grip on her arms. 'No, I didn't mean that,' she stammered.

'Then what is your meaning?'

'Only that I am not deciding to marry anyone at present. I need time. I haven't known you for very long.'

'But I needed to know you for only a few hours to know that you are the one dearest to my heart.'

Averil wanted to smile at this flowery speech, trying to imagine the same words from Connall's lips, but that would have been ludicrous.

When she remained silent, he continued, 'In any case, you have known the Englishman for only the same time.'

She nodded agreement. She was afraid to say that the length of acquaintanceship with a man was not always a criterion to the depth of one's feelings, but that would only reinforce Don Rodrigo's arguments as to his own sudden plunge into love for her.

Now he released her and hoisted her into her horse's saddle. For a while Averil and Don Rodrigo rode in silence, she busy with her thoughts, mostly concerning Connall, and no doubt her escort grieving over her present lack of responsive ardour.

When they were within half a mile of the villa, he said, 'I have a plan to offer you.' She jerked her attention to his words, apprehensive of some new arrangements he would try to make to take her to Madrid or Seville or somewhere else.

'Yes?' she prompted.

'You know the piece of my land which is, or will be, cut off when the new road is finished?'

'I know where it is.'

'I will give you this piece of land to add to your own estate. It is small and of not much value to me, but it would make a better addition to yours.'

She remembered from the maps this small triangle of land which adjoined the Serena estate. 'But I must remind you, Don Rodrigo, that I don't own the estate. It belongs to my relative. I am here only on her behalf.'

'Of course. Yet you must see that it would be an advantage. In a small way, it would compensate for the fact that the road cuts the Serena property almost in half.'

'Thank you for the offer,' said Averil. 'I must think about it.'

'Naturally. My lawyers will draw up the documents and there will be nothing for you—or the Serena estate,—to pay. No costs or anything of the sort.'

'It's very generous of you, Don Rodrigo,' she assured him, yet she tried to keep her tone matter-of-fact and businesslike, for she was not sure how generous he was trying to be. A sprat to catch a mackerel? What would he want in return?

In a short time she was in the villa patio and he helped her to dismount, availing himself a second time of the chance to hold her in his arms for a moment or two.

She thanked him for her lesson in horsemanship. 'You will make a splendid horsewoman,' he told her, his dark eyes warm with admiration. 'That will be useful and desirable in the future, for all the women of our family must ride well.'

She merely smiled an answer. Yet again, he was leaping forward into that future which might be all mapped out to him, but to her was still veiled in uncertainty.

'Our horses are at your disposal,' he continued, 'whenever you want to ride again. Perhaps tomorrow?'

'I would prefer the next day.' Consecutive days of riding with Don Rodrigo might easily constitute a habit which would be difficult to break when the need arose.

She found, too, when she walked upstairs that she was slightly more stiff than she had anticipated. She needed a day in between to get over her aches.

Naturally, it was almost no time before Connall had heard of her outing on horseback with Don Rodrigo. He called later in the day to talk to Gonzalo. When the two men had finished their conversation, Gonzalo told Averil that Señor Connall would like her to join him in the patio.

Averil dawdled a few moments. She must school herself not to rush out there at the gallop when Connall called, although she would readily have hastened on wings.

Connall was lounging almost full length in a long cane chair and untwined his long legs to stand up when she arrived on the covered part of the patio.

He poured her a glass of wine from the stone jug on the table.

'And what news?' he inquired.

'Has your spy system collapsed?' she countered. 'Why ask when you already know everything that has happened here in the last two or three days?'

'I like confirmation. It might be wrong to accept hearsay. The only points I know are that Don Rodrigo is back from Madrid and the pair of you went horse-riding this morning.'

She grinned. 'True. You need not sack your spy yet.'

'Don't need to. I saw you both with my own eyes.'

'Oh? Doing you own spying?' she laughed.

'I nearly rode over to your route, but I was busy and couldn't really spare the time to do a young Lochinvar act, snatch you off your mount and ride away with you like a pirate.'

She almost said, 'I wish you had!' but prevented that ridiculous phrase from leaving her lips.

'What was it you wanted to see me about?' she asked.

His hazel eyes widened. 'It's gone out of my head now. Must I have a reason for wanting to see you?'

'You're sounding like Don Rodrigo now,' she scoffed, then was immediately contrite, for she had not intended to belittle the Spaniard and, further than that, had landed herself in a trap which Connall lost no time in seizing upon.

'In what way?' Connall demanded.

'Oh, I only meant'—she waved her hand casually as though to blow the words away—'I meant that it sounded rather like some of his flattering speeches.'

He stared at her, gleams of malicious amusement in his eyes. 'A high old time you and Don Rodrigo have together, I'll warrant,' he said at last. 'He doing the flattering and you doing the simpering.'

'I never simper!' she protested.

He roared with laughter. 'I thought that would nettle you!'

She pushed his wineglass towards him. 'If all you've come for is to provoke me, you'd better drink up your wine and go.'

He picked up the glass and smiled at her. 'Inhospitable! Never do that in Spain. You must learn better than that if you're going to join one of the noble families of these parts.'

'Who says I am?'

He shrugged, finished his wine and set down the glass on the slatted wooden table. 'You remember I told you about the egg harvest they do in the marshes in the spring? Well, a party of men are coming from Sanlucar tomorrow. Would you like to see it?'

Yet again, his lightning change of mood astonished her.

She stifled her irritation. 'Yes, I'd like to see what goes on.'

'That's better,' he murmured. 'All sunny smiles again.'

She could cheerfully have slapped his face.

When she walked a few steps with him to the gates, it occurred to her to mention Don Rodrigo's offer of his small piece of land.

Instantly the bantering expression left Connall's face and he spoke seriously. 'What's he up to, I wonder? Is it merely a little present for a nice girl or is there something else behind it?'

'I pointed out,' Averil told him, 'that the estate is still my great-aunt's. Would it be an advantage to have that triangle?'

'It would—if the land were really worth anything, but he's known for a long time about the road and that plot has been neglected. Go down and have a good look at it soon.'

'Yes, I will, but Don Rodrigo will probably want to know soon if I can accept—on behalf of my great-aunt, of course.'

'Don't decide anything too rashly. These matters need considering. Besides, you might always gain time by telling him that you must also consult your lawyer in Seville.'

They were at the gate now and he turned towards her. 'Leave it for the moment and we'll talk about it again tomorrow.' He put his hand on her arm with what should have been a comforting gesture, but to her it was an exciting thrill, for it sent shivers of delight running up and down her spine.

After he had gone she calmed herself down, but at the same time she was conscious that she had achieved a new kind of relationship with him. In spite of his teasing and barbed comments, she believed that in a crisis he would prove a trustworthy friend. The real snag was that Averil did not want him only as a trustworthy friend. She was too deeply in love with him to be satisfied with that aspect. Yet she was in an impossible position, knowing hopelessly that the dream would never come true, the dream that one day Connall would look at her with love in his eyes.

CHAPTER SEVEN

WHEN Connall had told Averil about the famous egg-harvest of Las Marismas, she had not clearly understood exactly what happened.

In his car as he drove south and then towards the banks of the Guadalquivir river, Connall explained that he had arranged to meet a party of boatmen coming from Sanlucar.

'But surely it's robbery to take the eggs from the nests of terns and coot,' she objected.

He chuckled. 'That bird population will never be wiped out. The men always leave plenty.'

Where the road eventually curved down to the river bank, Connall left his car and he and Averil waited for the boat to arrive.

This was another aspect of the Spanish countryside that Averil had not so far seen. The morning sun glittered on the water and far away to the west the horizon was marked by scattered pine forests. Up river the limitless expanse of green and gold marsh stretched into misty distance.

'There's no amethyst light on the meadows this morning,' she remarked.

Connall turned towards her with an interested glance. 'I really believe you're coming to terms with this kind of landscape at last.'

'I admit it grows on one. At first——'

'At first you were determined to see nothing but the eternal rain,' he finished for her. 'But now you've seen for yourself that we have lovely springs and baking hot summers.'

'At least it has stopped raining,' she conceded with a grin. 'You do really like this part of Spain, don't you?'

'It's the wild life that attracts me. This area is unique in Europe. It changes so much with the seasons. In winter ducks and geese, then the avocets and herons, kites, vultures —all sorts. Unfortunately there are plans to try to drain

114

some of the swamps by means of dams and so on, and turn the entire area into agricultural land.'

'And that will mean the end of the wild life for the birds?' she queried.

'Perhaps not entirely. A small portion is already being conserved and administered by a trust. That's the part that's called Coto Doñana. It's more to the west and nearer the coast. You should go there one day.'

But now the still air throbbed to a distant rhythm of a motor-driven boat and soon a fairly large green boat with a yellow eye painted on the prow came in sight and steered towards the bank.

Connall picked up Averil bodily in his arms and sloshed through the shallow water to deposit her unceremoniously in the boat among half a dozen men. In the midst of the morning greetings and nods and 'Buenos dias', she hoped it would be wholly necessary to lift her out of the boat and put her ashore in like manner, for she had been delighted by that momentary cradling in Connall's arms, although she tried to stifle such rapture.

She noticed that a small skiff was lashed along one side of the boat and when the river narrowed to enter the marshes, three of the men launched the skiff and one man jumped into it, taking a long pole with him.

Evidently this was the signal for a bottle of wine to be passed round, and someone unearthed a small chipped glass for Averil's portion.

She was more intent on watching the egg-gatherer as he poled from one floating nest to another, scooping up dozens of eggs, but never apparently leaving a nest entirely empty. When the skiff was almost filled to sinking point with the load of rough straw baskets full of terns' and coots' eggs, he returned to the main boat to trans-ship his freight, before setting off again in a different direction.

At all times in the intervals of wine-drinking, the men shouted encouragement to the sole worker among the nests and Averil asked Connall if that was their only share of the labour.

He grinned. 'Perhaps he asked one companion to come

along and help and the rest of them joined in for company's sake.'

'Do they sell the eggs?' she asked.

'Oh, yes, for food. People in the towns are very eager to buy them. I'm not keen on the taste myself, but many others regard them as delicacies.'

Connall shared in the chatter of the men and once or twice one of them would address a remark to Averil, but her Spanish was not yet able to cope with the unfamiliar accents and Connall had to translate for her.

One smiled and pointed to Averil's fair hair contrasted against Connall's dark brown and announced that such widely disparate features would make a good match.

Averil understood these words only too well and she blushed, but Connall tossed the innuendo aside easily enough with, 'Every time they see me with a girl, they're always heading me straight for matrimony.'

'How many girls have you brought on the egg-harvests, then?' she wanted to know.

He gave her a sideways grin. 'Believe it or not, you're the first. I've seen it only once before myself.'

'H'm,' she murmured. 'Evidently they know about all your other acquaintances in Sanlucar or Cadiz.'

But now the man in the skiff was returning with his last load of baskets to transfer into the large boat which was now filled to capacity. The encouraging onlookers finished their sole task of hauling the skiff aboard and then settled in a small group in the stern, tucking their feet out of the way of the vulnerable piles of eggs.

The outboard motor chugged as the boat headed downstream but the steersman forgot the exact spot where Connall and Averil had boarded the boat and shot some distance farther down before he slowed speed and approached the bank. This time Averil's anticipatory delight in the prospect of Connall's lifting her out was immediately quelled, for one of the men clambered over the bow, grasped her hands and swung her on to more or less dry land. Connall was still gossiping with the other men, but eventually thanked them and vaulted over the bow to join Averil. The substitute, she reflected, was not the same.

116

'It's only a short walk to where I left the car,' Connall explained.

But the car had disappeared.

He looked about and scratched his head. 'I could have sworn this was the place.'

'It looks the same to me,' she assured him. 'Here are the tyre marks.'

'And our footprints? Let's see if they fit.'

As they tried to fit their shod feet into the slight indentations in the moist sandy ground, Averil jostled against him, then drew sharply away. He must not imagine that she was deliberately bumping into him and pretending to lose her balance.

'Well, some funny things have happened to me in my time,' he exploded, 'but I've never known my car vanish into thin air in an unpopulated park like this. In towns, yes, the police might have removed it, but——'

'What do we do now?' she asked mildly.

'Well, we haven't a magic lamp to rub so that a genie will appear and present us with a brand-new automobile,' he returned impatiently. He sat down on an adjacent piece of rock. 'Let's see. The nearest house was about two miles back. We must walk there and try to telephone if possible.'

With a boat trip in mind, Averil had put on canvas sandals which were not suitable for walking along the rough, boulder-strewn road, but she knew Connall would despise her if she complained.

'I wish we'd gone right down to Sanlucar with the men,' said Connall. 'We could have had a meal there and worried about the car later.'

Averil realised that she was hungry, but there was no point in saying so.

The house was not much more than a shack, painted bright terra-cotta and surrounded by a broken wooden fence.

Connall marched boldly to the only door he could see, but no one came in response to his determined knocking. 'I'll go around the back. You'd better come with me,' he said.

Chickens flew across the yard and a small boy sleeping in

a patch of shade raised himself on one elbow at the entrance of strangers.

Connall spoke rapidly in Spanish to the boy, who shook his head. In a moment a woman came hurrying out of a shed and Connall repeated his inquiries.

The woman's attitude changed instantly. She clasped her hands nervously and seemed about to fall on her knees in front of Connall. As far as Averil could understand the gist of the broken, incoherent conversation, it seemed that someone was ill and had been taken in the car to the nearest village.

The woman was evidently trying to placate Connall, wringing her hands, the tears rolling down her cheeks. Then she beckoned to him to follow her into the little house.

Before he complied, Connall turned towards Averil. 'Well, I'm damned! Whoever it is has helped himself to my car and shot off with it to a doctor. Heaven knows when I shall see it again—if ever. Probably already lying in a ditch or an *ojo*.'

Averil had already learned that the word '*ojo*' which Connall had previously used in derision meant neither 'eye' nor 'keyhole' but indicated a treacherous waterhole into which a man, an animal or a car could sink and be lost.

She followed Connall into the house, where the woman bade them sit at a table, scrubbed to a hygienic whiteness. She produced bread, a platter of cold meat and a jug of wine and invited them to eat.

Averil was reluctant, although really hungry. 'Should we really take the food?' she asked Connall in English. 'They can't afford it.'

Connall smiled. 'You will offend a Spanish woman if you don't accept. Eat and be thankful.'

A few minutes later he said to Averil, 'She thinks they will shortly be back with the car—whoever they are, so we must wait.'

It was an hour later before the sound of a car bumping along the uneven roadway came to their ears.

Connall shot out of the house and when Averil followed, stopping to place a little money secretly in the folds of the tablecloth, she found Connall arguing furiously with a

118

middle-aged man standing by the car.

'But, *señor*!' the man pleaded, 'I could not leave my father to die!' That much Averil could understand, but the two men launched into rapid Spanish which she could not follow.

Eventually Connall calmed himself and began to examine the car for possible damage. A quarter of an hour later, he and Averil were driving along the rough road back to the crossroads on the way home.

'I suppose I'm partly to blame,' he admitted. 'I left the ignition key in and I didn't lock the doors, but then I didn't suppose a soul would come along and drive off. Careless of me.'

'And why did the man take it?' queried Averil. 'Was his father ill?'

'Apparently, so he told me, the father works on the other side of the river as a bull breeder, and some days ago he was injured by a fiery young bull. The wound became worse and the son went across to fetch his father and take him to a doctor in the next village.' Connall now smiled at the recollection of the altercation with the Spaniard only a short time ago.

'I'm not unsympathetic,' he continued, 'but that man must have thought providence had answered his prayers and presented him with a car just when he needed it. You see, in the meantime we had arrived and then gone off in the boat upriver.'

'He was lucky. What else would he have done if your car hadn't been there?'

'I asked him that,' replied Connall, 'and he said—and I really believe him—that he would have had to bring a donkey down to the river and let his father ride the six or seven miles to the village.'

'I'm glad the car was there to save the old man all that pain and trouble,' murmured Averil.

'That's something I like about the Spanish people. In the main they're absolutely honest. That son intended to drive the car right down to the water's edge where I left it. I stopped him before he could go past the shack. Elsewhere, someone who borrows a car thinks nothing of abandoning it

119

when the vehicle has served his purpose.' After a pause, he added, 'I'm speaking, of course, only about the ordinary Spanish folk. Noblemen like Don Rodrigo don't always have such high motives. Which reminds me—about that strip of land you spoke about——'

'I shall look at the piece tomorrow,' promised Averil.

'I'm still wondering what he wants in return. Is it to soften you up, do you think?'

His eyes held mischief again.

'I'm not butter that needs to be taken off the chill,' she protested indignantly.

'Taken off the chill,' he echoed in a mock sage tone. 'A good expression. I'm hoping that you *are* on the chilly side to him.'

'Why should you hope that?' she asked, hope springing again against her will that he might be even slightly jealous of Don Rodrigo's attentions to her.

'Why? Only because I don't want to see you bowled over by an undeniably handsome Don. Whatever he says, however flattering, you have to remember that it's most unlikely that he would marry an English girl.'

'And suppose I were bowléd over,' she murmured in a quiet voice, 'what would you do to save me?'

'Nothing at all. Having warned you on more than one occasion, it wouldn't be my responsibility to pull your fingers out of the flame when you burnt them.'

'I suppose you'd stand by and laugh?'

'No. I might take care to be over the hills and far away.'

A chill crept into her being at these words. He was an impossible man to pin down. Any girl who came into contact with him must be determined to enjoy his companionship when he chose to give it and wave him goodbye when he decided to wing away to another area where other girls would listen to his often ambiguous words and watch for the tender glances to come their way.

On arrival at the Villa Serena, Connall carried the basket of eggs which was his share of the harvesting loot and which he had humped all the way from the riverbank to the shack where he had waited for his car. Now he took the

England, she knew, there would be many other

eggs towards the kitchen to give Marta, but one of the younger girls came out hurriedly, babbling *'Señor, señor, telegrama, telegrama!'*

'What telegram?' he asked.

But the telegram was for Averil. As she read the words, the colour drained from her face and the world receded far away.

'Bad news?'

Connall's voice recalled her. She thrust the telegram into his hand.

'My great-aunt Freda,' she explained to Marta, a few moments later, 'is very ill and I must return to England as soon as possible.'

'Come outside,' advised Connall, no doubt aware of the several pairs of inquisitive eyes in the kitchen.

He led Averil out to the patio and sat opposite her. In a few moments someone brought a glass of brandy for her to sip.

'Is she very old?' asked Connall quietly.

'No. Only in her early sixties, but she's badly crippled by arthritis. She may possibly have had a fall recently. I don't know.' Averil took a sip of brandy and felt it revive her composure. 'She would have been delighted to come here if she could have managed the travelling. I think she had always retained in her mind a vision of what Spain was like, right from the time when Don Francisco wanted to marry her.'

'But don't you think she would have been disappointed to find the reality so far below her expectations—just as you were disappointed when you first came here?'

'I expect so, but I've overcome that.'

'Her disappointment might have lasted longer and shattered her dream,' Connall pointed out gently. 'But we must be practical. You can't fly tonight, but you could go on the midday plane. I'll go up to my place and telephone for a flight reservation. It's time you had your own phone reinstated,' he added with a touch of asperity.

She needed that slightly cold douche more than sympathy, for if he had spoken too soothingly, she would have collapsed on to his shoulder with weeping.

'I've asked several times for the phone to be reconnected, but it's not been done,' she said.

'I'll come back and let you know what I can fix up,' he promised, and was off across the patio to his car.

For a few moments Averil, left to herself, was in a trance-like state of stupefaction, but then she reminded herself there was no time to lose. Packing to be done, instructions for Gonzalo about money matters, instructions to Marta on household concerns, a dozen items to attend to.

In her bedroom she roamed about gathering her clothes and possessions, wondering whether she ought to take everything with her on the assumption that she would not be returning to the Villa Serena. Was this the end of the Spanish adventure? If Great-aunt Freda died, there was no likelihood that Averil would inherit more than a small share, certainly not the Serena estate. If, on the other hand, Great-aunt Freda recovered, there was at least a possibility that Averil might come back to continue the legal fight.

Averil had brought only a modest amount of luggage with her in the first place and had added very little to it, but now she decided to travel back with only one essential suitcase, leaving the rest of her possessions as a kind of hostage to the hope that her great-aunt would recover.

Connall returned in a couple of hours and stayed to dinner at the villa. He had booked the flight for her and told her the time of arrival in England, so that she could be met by some member of her family.

During his absence it had occurred to Averil that in all the time she had known him, she had never discovered where he lived or in what circumstances.

As they sat together on the patio after dinner, alone with coffee and brandy and Connall in a relaxed attitude from which she took her cue, trying to match his manner, she asked the question now. 'Whereabouts do you live in the village?'

'I lodge in a stone cottage with an old crone who looks after me as though I were her grandson, which she often calls me.'

'But where is it?' she persisted, trying to visualise him indoors.

122

'You wouldn't find it unless I took you there. Up a small alley and at the top of an outside stairway, usually inhabited by cats. I haven't a permanent home anywhere; I roam about too much and I'm usually too far from hotels, which I dislike anyway. I don't usually have enough time to settle in one place or surround myself with creature comforts. Clothes, a few books, no more than I can pack into the car.'

'A nomadic existence,' she murmured.

'That's right. So I try not to put down roots anywhere. It becomes too painful when you pull them up again.'

Even in the midst of her distress and her imminent departure to England, she realised that once again he was warning her not to expect any attachment on his part; even more than that, he was telling her that it would be futile for her to form any attachment to him. His words were plainly spoken and a girl would be a fool who thought otherwise.

Consequently, when he took his leave and she accompanied him across the patio towards his car, she was all the more astonished at his actions which completely, so it seemed, belied his words. In the shadow of a clump of bushes, his arms closed around her in an embrace that took her by surprise, but was none the less exquisite in its rapture. As he kissed her with a passion that shook her frame, she was conscious of the thought that this was what she had waited for. She scarcely heard his murmured endearments, but a few words caught her attention. '... I'm sorry you're going ... we could have ... but in the end it's for the best ... you'll soon forget me ... I can't marry you ...' Then he was thrusting her away from him so roughly that she tottered to regain her balance.

Connall moved rapidly to his car, then flung over his shoulder, 'I'll call about nine o'clock tomorrow morning to drive you to the airport.'

Averil watched him drive away and stood there numb, frozen with the dull ache of parting. With the stiffness of an automaton, eventually she walked indoors and up to her room. Hunched on the bed, she asked the empty air why, oh, why did he have to sweep her up to the heights of

123

ecstasy only to dash her down again with sickening brutality?

She tried to remember his words, but the two recurring phrases which beat in her brain were '... you'll soon forget me ... I can't marry you'.

She would never be able to forget Connall. Wherever she went or whoever she met, he would remain a part of her life, an interlude perhaps that she would recall with some pleasure and intense pain. No doubt the pleasure would endure and the pain would soften in the course of time.

Then what was the underlying meaning of those words— '... I can't marry you'. That an insurmountable obstacle stood in the way? That he was married already, parted from a wife in England or elsewhere? Averil realised how little she knew of Connall's background. He had never mentioned any part of England to which he belonged or where he had lived before coming to Spain.

But it occurred to her that perhaps his words had a different implication, that she was not the kind of girl he could ever marry, not his type, not the one who would surrender the possibility of a life accompanied by modern comforts in order to share his kind of nomadic existence.

She sprang up off the bed, wanting to cry out aloud that she was just that girl! If he offered her the chance, she would willingly tramp about Spain or the rest of Europe or wherever his profession demanded. Other women were glad to make a home in bleak surroundings for the sake of the men they loved. Why should Connall deprive her of that choice?

She finished packing the single suitcase she had decided to take, but was now uncertain if that was a wise move. Could she bear to return for any reason to the Serena estate and renew a tenuous relationship with Connall when he had now evidently determined that such a passing friendship on his part was already in the past, neatly terminated with an affectionate goodbye kiss?

She tried to concentrate on the point, but her thoughts constantly veered to Connall's whispered words. Eventually she found herself collecting all her possessions and filling a second suitcase. Whatever the condition of her great-aunt, there would be no point in returning here. Better to make a clean break and write off this unhappy chapter as experience.

She was up early, for sleep was too difficult, and when she was dressed she went downstairs and out into the patio. Beyond the gates she walked a short distance along the road from which she could see the wide spaces of the marsh meadows, patched with the masses of white and grey birds covering the large dry places, the bright green of the grassy areas, dotted with horses and cattle grazing.

She looked in vain for that amethyst light which imbued the swamplands with a lovely mysterious radiance, but the dawn was pink and golden as the sun came up in a clear sky. Perhaps she would never see the meadows again in that amethyst glow.

When she returned to the villa she found that Don Rodrigo was already there. He took her hands and held them sympathetically in his own.

'I am so sorry you have to go away because of bad news,' he said. 'Naturally your family is important and you must return to England, but I hope you will come back here at the earliest moment.'

Sudden tears sprang to Averil's eyes. The contrast between Connall's ruthless rejection of her last night and Don Rodrigo's kindly attentions was too much. She struggled to regain her composure and managed to smile at Don Rodrigo.

'Thank you,' she murmured. 'How did you know I had to leave this morning?'

He inclined his head and smiled. 'Sometimes it is good to have people who will pass on messages, whether good or bad.'

Averil supposed that as usual Vanna had been the news-carrier. Perhaps in this instance the girl had been of some benefit, for now Averil saw salvation in Don Rodrigo's early call. She had been dreading meeting Connall again after last night's emotional scene and considered it was doubly cruel of him to promise in so casual a manner to take her to the airport this morning.

'Could you drive me to Seville to catch the plane?' she

125

now asked Don Rodrigo.

'But of course. That is why I am here so early. What time?'

'I should like to start soon after eight o'clock.' She looked at her watch and saw that it was barely seven o'clock, so that would give time for breakfast and the last farewells. She must be away well before nine when Connall would probably come.

'Is your reservation made?' asked Don Rodrigo.

'Yes.' After a pause she added, 'Connall telephoned last night.'

'So he was here when——?'

'When the telegram arrived. Well, actually the telegram had come earlier in the afternoon, but I was out.'

Don Rodrigo's face fell and became gloomy. 'I am grieved that you spent the day with the Englishman. Your last day here.'

She managed a smile. 'No one could know that. You'll remember that I promised to come riding with you this morning.'

'I had not forgotten. Did you think I had? Well, it is something very agreeable to be driving you to Seville instead, although it is for a sad occasion. At least I shall have the privilege of bidding you farewell.'

That was the haunting dread that had been in Averil's mind since last night—that Connall might repeat his pseudo-passionate caresses at the airport.

During the drive to Seville, Averil kept the conversation on a mild, friendly note, but she was quite surprised when she found that Don Rodrigo was accompanying her in the plane from Seville to Madrid where she would change.

'It's very good of you,' she thanked him, 'but it wasn't necessary.'

'Not necessary, perhaps,' he agreed, 'but very desirable. I am filled with sorrow that you have to go back to England, so I must come as far as possible with you. But you will return when your great-aunt is better? Without you, my life will be everlasting torment.'

His flattering, flowery words grated on Averil in her present unhappy state. Yet his intentions were amiable and

126

far from the ironic expressions that Connall would have used in similar circumstances. But she refused to let her mind dwell on Connall. There would be long stretches of aching emptiness ahead of her when this man to whom she had so foolishly given her heart would fill the blank spaces in her mind.

Don Rodrigo's farewells at Madrid had been protracted and tender, but at airports this was hardly noticeable. The plane was crossing the northern coast of Spain before Averil could allow herself to snap her restraint and seek refuge behind the pages of a magazine while the slow tears coursed down her cheeks.

At London Airport a message from her father awaited her and she telephoned her home number.

'She's very ill,' her father told her. 'It's her heart. Can you manage to get down here by yourself? It's rather difficult for us—and such short notice.'

'Oh, don't worry,' she assured her father. 'I can cope quite well. I'll get the earliest train I can.'

'Good. Someone will be at the station to meet you at this end,' her father promised. 'Take care of yourself, love.'

It was her sister Dinah who had a taxi waiting outside the station at home.

'What a pity you had to come home like this,' the girl exclaimed. 'Weren't you heartbroken to leave Spain?'

Averil was watching her luggage being stowed into the taxi. The word 'heartbroken' had an ironic sound to it, but she answered Dinah lightly. 'Not exactly heartbroken. Sorry, perhaps, to leave such an interesting part of the country.'

'And interesting friends, too?' persisted Dinah.

'Yes, I made some friends there,' Averil replied guardedly.

'Tell me about them,' begged her sister.

'Later, darling. I'm not in the mood just now.'

'Oh, yes, of course. Poor Great-aunt Freda. Such a waste! She could have had a happy life—in Spain, of all places—but she had to throw it all away and then put up with pain and suffering.' The younger girl's voice held such a note of sympathy that again Averil's eyes were bright

127

with tears which she blinked back hastily before arriving at her home.

In the house there was a flurry of excitement in welcoming Averil and then arranging visits to the hospital next morning.

'How serious is it?' she asked her mother.

Mrs. Sanderson shook her head gravely. 'Very serious, dear. We wouldn't have cabled the news to you if the attack had been only slight. But we thought you ought to know—and then decide for youself whether you returned here or not.'

'I'm glad I've come home,' said Averil, and was aware of her mother's sharp questioning look.

At the hospital next day Averil realised that her great-aunt was very weak.

'You mustn't tire her,' the nurse enjoined Averil. 'Only ten minutes, please.'

Even in her weakness, Great-aunt Freda displayed the courage she had shown all her life.

'Averil, listen,' she whispered urgently, but so softly that Averil had to bend down to hear. 'Did you like Spain?'

The question was unexpected. Averil answered bravely, 'Yes, I did, although it was so different from what I expected. I wrote to you all about it.'

'Yes, I know. But if you think you can find happiness there, go back and seize it. I let my chance slip away, but you must *not* do that.'

The effort of speaking seemed almost too much for the frail woman in the bed.

'Are you all right?' asked Averil anxiously. 'Shall I ring for the nurse?'

'No, no. I must finish. There were so many times when I longed to see Spain just once—for the sake of the man who loved me. I loved him, too—but circumstances were too strong for me, or perhaps I was a coward.'

'No, never that,' contradicted Averil softly.

'So if you go—and perhaps stay there—I shall feel that you've gone there in my place. Be happy, child.'

There was a long pause and Averil waited, unwilling to disturb her great-aunt's train of thought.

'It is not impossible to find happiness with a man of a different nationality,' the older woman whispered. 'Difficult sometimes, but where there is love——' her voice trailed away and a serene smile played about her lips.

In her letters Averil had mentioned Don Rodrigo, particularly in matters of business, the visits to Seville, the fact that his estate adjoined the Serena property, but she was thankful now that she had never written of Connall.

'Thank you, dear, for all you've done on the legal side,' continued her great-aunt. 'Perhaps one day the estate will be prosperous and flourishing, thanks to you.'

Here again, Averil was glad that she had not so far mentioned the rival claimant, Renata. At the time she had considered it more prudent to wait until Renata's claim was more fully established.

The tears sprang again to Averil's eyes. A prosperous and flourishing estate, maybe—but she would never see it.

Then the nurse was at Averil's elbow. 'Please, you must go now,' she murmured.

Averil embraced Great-aunt Freda, desperately trying not to believe that it might be the last time, and with an affectionate smile to the woman in the bed, she tiptoed out of the room.

In the evening when their mother had gone to the hospital, Averil and Dinah talked in subdued tones. Dinah was anxious to learn as much as possible about the Spanish scene.

'What is he like, this Spaniard you've met there? Don Rodrigo. Is he tall, dark and handsome?'

Averil smiled. 'Yes, you could say that he's all of those.'

Yet a vision came before her inward eye of the man who was tall, but not so dark and certainly considerably less handsome than Don Rodrigo. When would she be free of this obsession that came into her mind on the slightest pretext?

'Do you think you'll go back to Spain and marry him?'

'Who?' Averil's thoughts, momentarily dreaming along a path she would prefer to forget, swerved back to her sister's question.

'Who?' echoed Dinah. 'Is there someone else then that

you haven't told us about?' She laughed. 'You see, that's what I told you before you went to Spain—that you'd be knee-deep in proposals from handsome Spaniards and English tourists and——'

'That part of Spain isn't exactly the place for English tourists,' broke in Averil, 'unless they're interested in the wild life conservation area.'

'What about this road that you wrote about, the one that cuts across the estate? Haven't you met anyone in that connection?'

'There's hardly anyone to meet—only a gang of workmen and a road engineer.'

Dinah wrinkled up her face in mild disgust. 'Nothing very exciting about those. No, my bet is on Don Rodrigo. Has he asked you to marry him?'

In spite of herself Averil coloured. She wanted to ridicule such a notion, but she could not make the lie convincing enough. 'Well, in a way,' she admitted.

'There! I knew it would be a romance,' broke in Dinah.

'Dinah, listen! There's nothing to get excited about. You must realise that all Spaniards—or most of them anyway—vow eternal devotion, make flowery speeches, give you the most exaggerated compliments, even say that they want to marry you, but it doesn't really mean anything. It's more than likely that Don Rodrigo's family has already chosen a bride for him, and almost certainly she'll be Spanish and of good family.'

'But you're a little bit in love with him?' Dinah persisted.

'Not really. I like him. He's very charming, but——'

'Then it's someone else you've met there. Averil, you're quite different from when you went away. I can always tell when you're hiding something. Come on, tell me.' Dinah's voice was coaxing, the way it had been when she was small and wanted favours from Averil.

Averil laughed lightly. 'There's nothing to tell. I think I heard Father come in.' She was relieved of a diversion to enable her to fend off Dinah's probing questions.

At breakfast next morning came the news that Great-aunt Freda had slipped away in her sleep.

'Your mother was there all night, but Freda just drifted away with a smile, she said.'

'How can we help, Father?' asked Averil. 'Shall we go to the hospital or stay here and let Mother rest?'

Mr. Sanderson smiled at his daughter. 'I daresay your mother would be glad of the chance to put her feet up. I'm going in a few minutes to fetch her.'

When the quiet funeral was over and the will disclosed, Averil found that she had been left the entire Serena estate.

'... if I have singled out Averil and perhaps shown some favouritism,' the will ran, 'it is because I believe she will acquire a love of Spain and find happiness there...'

Averil was overwhelmed by the bequest and discussed the matter with her father later that night.

'You could arrange to sell it,' he suggested. 'Perhaps this Don Rodrigo would buy. You say his own property runs alongside. Might be convenient for him, although he might not give you a very good price if he wants to be businesslike. He'll know that you don't particularly want to be tied to the place.'

'I'll think about it, Father,' Averil promised. 'In any case, there will be fresh legal matters to settle before I could offer the villa and estate to Don Rodrigo.'

At the end of a week she knew that she was compelled to return to Spain, no matter on what pretext. That wild, lonely marshland beckoned her irresistibly. Whether she ever saw Connall again or was effusively welcomed by Don Rodrigo did not matter; she must visit the Villa Serena and stay there for at least a while, gaze on the curious mauve haze at sunset that turned the meadows to amethyst. Great-aunt Freda had understood Averil's longing and had lovingly and cleverly dangled the bait by bequeathing the girl the entire estate.

Averil told her father of her decision. 'There's also this complication of another person claiming, Renata. I doubt if I could really leave this to the lawyers to straighten out.'

Her father nodded. 'Yes, I can see that in your absence

the other party's case might be strengthened. But, my dear Averil, why do you want what you say is a derelict villa and a badly neglected estate?'

Averil was thoughtful for a few moments. 'I feel that I'd be letting Freda down if I allowed the property to drift away into other hands without at least making a fight for it.'

While Mr. Sanderson seemed to accept Averil's decision, Dinah was openly scornful in a teasing, younger-sister way.

'I knew there was a great attraction there,' she declared. 'This Don Rodrigo? Or someone else? What about that road engineer? Is he young?'

Averil laughed. 'I suppose you could call him youngish, but——'

'Then let me advise you,' continued Dinah pompously. 'Don't tangle yourself with roadmen. Concentrate on Don Rodrigo. After all, if you marry him and he has a big house and lots of servants and lives in luxury, I shall expect to come to you for visits and holidays. Goodness, that would be something to boast about at school! Oh, yes, I'm just off to Spain to visit my brother-in-law, the Count of—whatever it is—he lives in a castle and——'

'Never say anything about castles in Spain,' advised Averil, 'or no one will believe a word!'

'All right. Tell me the right word,' urged Dinah.

'What does it matter when it won't happen that way?' queried Averil.

Dinah sighed deeply. 'Glamorous events and possibilities are wasted on you. Now if I were in your place——'

'Then wait a few years and perhaps you might be glad that I did what I could to rescue the property. Think how that would go down with your school chums! I'm just back from visiting my family estate and vineyards in Spain ...'

Dinah laughed and thrust an arm affectionately around Averil's shoulders. 'You win! But don't you dare do anything secretly. No hole-and-corner wedding, mind. I want to be there to see the grand ceremony.'

'If I did marry Don Rodrigo, how do you know the quite simple ceremony wouldn't be here in our local church?'

Dinah's face momentarily fell. 'Oh, no! You might as

132

well marry anyone—even an old road man. No, it must be in Spain with all the pomp and panoply that I'm sure they know how to do.'

'All right. I promise to let you know if there's a grand occasion, but you're in for a disappointment, and don't blame me.'

Averil, in the midst of her packing and other arrangements for her flight to Spain, reflected that this time she was preparing for a long stay at the Villa Serena. Two new suitcases were added to the luggage list and she invested in several new outfits, a couple of trouser suits with shirts and sweaters, two full-length summer dresses that could be worn for dancing or dining out.

What am I doing, rushing back like this to the very place that has given me so much pain? Yet the answer was that she had no choice. A certain sense of loyalty to Great-aunt Freda demanded that her legacy should not be allowed to slip through Averil's fingers or be handed by default to Renata. But beyond that, the overwhelming reason was that Averil was drawn to Las Marismas as though by a magnet and the compelling power belonged to Connall. Even if she never saw him again, Averil convinced herself that she must re-visit the Villa Serena, walk about the estate, tread the paths where she had walked with him. Then perhaps she would be able to eradicate this anguished longing for a man to whom she meant nothing. She would dutifully attend to all the legal matters, decide what should be done with the estate, sell it or place it in the hands of a competent manager. Then she would leave Spain and never again visit the country where she had so wholly and foolishly lost her heart.

CHAPTER EIGHT

On arrival in Seville, Averil decided to spend the night there, so that she could visit the notary's office next day and hand him the various documents she had brought with her from England, entitling her to the estate as an inheritance.

Established in a hotel not far from the Calle de los Sierpes, Averil smiled at her own self-deception. Although it might be important to see the lawyer, she knew she was deliberately making herself pause before that final stage of the journey to the Villa Serena. All the time since she had left her home, on the train journey, then the plane to Madrid, thence to Seville, she had been aware of this heady sense of elation as though she were an expatriate now returning to a beloved homeland.

She had not informed Don Rodrigo of her impending return, preferring to see him in her own villa, rather than be met at Seville. She hesitated about letting Gonzalo and Marta know of her arrival, but if she advised them, the news would instantly reach Don Rodrigo via Vanna or someone else.

In the lawyer's office next day, Averil was surprised by Señor Navarro's enthusiastic attitude. The notary expressed his pleasure at the fact that Averil was now the legal owner of the estate, when her claim could be proved satisfactorily, and that of Renata dismissed.

'This is so much better to deal with the real owner, you understand, *señorita*,' he told her. 'Now I am sure we shall be able to move fast and settle all the details.'

While he explained the documents it occurred to her that the question of the valuable books owned by Don Francisco had never been solved.

Señor Navarro shook his head when she mentioned the subject. 'No books were brought here from Don Francisco's villa. You must remember that it is at least *possible* that he sold them during his lifetime.'

'Perhaps he did,' agreed Averil, 'and it is no use looking

134

for them.'

Later in the day she was able to hire without difficulty a car to take her to the Villa Serena. Perhaps, she reflected, her improved Spanish held a more authoritative note.

The evening was still daylight when the car drove into the patio and the first object that attracted her attention was a large swinging hammock piled with cushions. As she looked more closely, Averil saw that the occupant of the hammock was Renata, who waved a languid hand in Averil's direction.

Averil was forced to attend to the car-driver and have her luggage transferred indoors. Almost immediately Marta came rushing towards Averil, full of incoherent apologies in a torrent of Spanish.

Averil assumed the woman was excusing herself because she had not known of Averil's arrival and was taken by surprise, but gradually the phrases began to make sense. The words 'Señorita Bonaventa' recurred many times, and now Averil saw that Renata had moved from the swinging hammock and was close by.

'You are surprised?' Renata queried.

'Why should I be surprised?' asked Averil.

Renata smiled. 'It was the best thing, so my lawyer told me. That I should come and live here.'

'Live here?' echoed Averil. 'But—but what right——? Oh, I see, you mean you are staying here for a time, even though——' She had been about to point out that Renata had not been invited, but thought it wiser not to aggravate what was already a tricky situation.

'Oh, no, I mean to live here all the time. It is my property. I am entitled to do so. And you, Señorita Averil, must be my guest—for a while.'

Averil opened her mouth to gasp that Renata was not lacking in impudence. 'We had better go indoors and discuss this matter,' she said as smoothly as she could manage.

In Averil's absence the sitting-room had not only been tidied, but refurnished with items from other rooms.

'Please sit down,' invited Renata.

'On the contrary, I prefer to stand,' declared Averil. 'I

135

must first tell you that——'

'Please do not let us be angry with each other,' coaxed Renata in her silkiest voice. 'I do not wish you to spend money on the lawyers' fees when you cannot succeed. You must realise that I, the niece of Don Francisco, have a greater claim than you, for it is only your aunt—or some relative that——'

'If you would allow me to finish,' broke in Averil hotly, 'I was about to tell you that the property is lawfully mine. My great-aunt Freda died a fortnight ago and she has bequeathed me the entire estate.'

Renata smiled and shrugged. 'It is not important. You are still not a relative of Don Francisco.'

'Are you sure that you are?' countered Averil, hardly knowing what made her ask the question.

Renata's dark eyes showed a momentary flicker of concern. 'But of course. My mother was Don Francisco's sister.'

'Then how is it that you have apparently never been here before? No visits to your uncle during all those years when you lived only as far as Cadiz? Did your mother visit him, or did he call on her?'

Renata shook her head slowly. 'There was some matter between them, a dispute, and my mother would not come here.'

Averil was silent and in a moment or two she sank into a chair, even then noting that this was a better upholstered article than had formerly graced this sitting-room.

The other girl's statements were fairly logical. Disputes arose between relatives and led to estrangements.

'What do you propose to do now?' she asked Renata.

'Nothing.' Renata smiled. 'I am in possession of the villa.'

'I doubt it,' snapped Averil. 'You can't yet prove your claim.'

'But can you?'

'Yes, I'm sure I can,' replied Averil firmly, although she felt far from certain. It depended now on whose side the lawyers were on, she thought. 'So, as the first claimant, I have the right to temporary possession.' She smiled at the

Spanish girl. 'And of course you must be my guest for a time,' she added, hoping that the irony of those repeated words was not lost on the other.

'We shall see,' promised Renata. 'In the meantime, I must make sure that you are comfortable. I will ask someone to take your luggage to your room. Naturally, we must dine together. You will not refuse?'

'Certainly not. I would have no reason for refusing to dine with my guest!' Averil tossed an exaggerated smile at Renata.

When, however, she went upstairs to her old room, she found that it had been denuded of at least half its furniture. Her suitcases were not here, either. She went out to the landing and called for Marta.

'What is the meaning of this?' she asked when the woman arrived. 'Most of my furniture seems to have disappeared.'

'It is a mistake. I have made another room ready for you,' explained Marta. 'Señorita Bonaventa asked for many alterations in the rooms.'

'And which is her bedroom?'

'That one.' Marta pointed to the large room which she and Gonzalo had shared in more recent times, but which was obviously the best room on that floor.

Averil made an exclamation of disgust. 'So she has already turned you and Gonzalo out of that room! That is something that I would never have done, except for a very special reason. Where is your room now?'

Marta indicated one along a corridor, which Averil knew to be fairly small.

'Then accept this for the time being, Marta, and we will rearrange everything later on. Please help me, Marta, by acknowledging me as the mistress of this house, and do not take orders from Señorita Bonaventa.'

Marta smiled nervously. 'Now that you are here, *señorita*, perhaps it will be easy, but before—you understand— we could not——'

'Of course I understand.' Averil touched the woman's arm with a reassuring gesture. 'Now show me which is my room now.'

When Marta had returned downstairs, Averil sat on the

137

bed, a less comfortable one she thought than her own, and pondered on the situation. If Connall were here, he would obviously soon put Renata in her place. But a second's more reflection doubted this. If he were attracted to Renata, he would not undermine her assured position in the house. In fact, he might even have given Renata the idea.

Averil rose quickly and walked about the room. Oh, if that were so—how could he behave in such an unspeakable manner?

She must obtain Don Rodrigo's aid, and speedily. The trusted grapevine system must already have informed him that Renata was in occupation. The message would soon filter through that Averil had returned. Yet it would be damaging, if not fatal, to ask for and accept favours from Don Rodrigo. His help in establishing her as owner might demand a price that Averil was not prepared to pay—or at least not yet. Also how could she be sure that he did not approve of a Spanish girl taking over the property? He might support Renata instead of Averil.

With a sigh, Averil unpacked one of her suitcases, noting that neither of the young maids had been sent up to do this for her. She showered and changed into one of her newer dresses, if only to give herself courage to face Renata across the dinner table.

'Now I must tell you all the news of what has happened during your absence,' Renata said complacently during the soup.

'Please do,' prompted Averil calmly.

'One horse has a new baby—what do you call?'

'A foal,' supplied Averil.

'Ah, yes, a foal. Gonzalo has some new tools for the vines.'

'Oh? What tools?'

Renata impatiently waved her hand. 'Tools! I do not know what they are for. They have long handles.'

'Hoes, probably. Go on.'

'There is nothing more. Life here is not interesting. Oh, yes, Don Rodrigo rode over one morning to ask if we had heard news from you in England. I told him that you had gone to England for ever and would not return.'

'You didn't know that,' protested Averil.

'But everyone thought so. You took all your luggage back with you. Nothing was left here,' pointed out Renata.

'That was only because I had no idea how long I might be required in England,' Averil asserted, but she knew there was a certain lameness in that reply. 'And have you seen Don Rodrigo again?'

Renata give her companion a self-satisfied smile. 'On several occasions. Sometimes we have been riding together. He is very charming and he has told me a great deal about his family.'

The idea floated into Averil's mind that perhaps Renata would prove a suitable diversion for Don Rodrigo, but as though the Spanish girl read her thoughts, Renata's next remark was clear enough. 'Naturally, you are eager to hear some news of the English *señor*. He came several times to my home in Cadiz.' Renata giggled and looked coquettish. 'In fact, it is difficult to keep him away. He was very much in favour of my coming to live here, because of course it is near where he is working.'

'Oh, is he still working on the same piece of road?' asked Averil casually, helping herself to salad. 'And does he now call here frequently to see you?'

Renata's dark eyes shone with glee. 'I can see that you are indeed jealous of his attentions to me, but I assure you that I have done so little to encourage him. It is not my fault if he should prefer a Spanish girl to an English one.'

Averil was aware of the underlying significance of that remark. In Renata's view, Connall could not fail to be more attracted to a dazzling Spanish beauty than to a milk-and-water miss like Averil.

Averil controlled herself enough to smile at Renata. 'No, indeed, we must all accept attentions from men as we find them—and not complain if the attraction does not last long.'

'You are a philosopher,' commented Renata.

'And you are not?' queried Averil teasingly. 'I would advise you to cultivate philosophy of that kind where Connall is concerned. I would not like to see you grieving and disappointed when he flits away to another flower.'

'Ah, you have already experienced a coolness on his part
—perhaps before you went to England?'

Averil almost choked, remembering that night when he
had kissed her so passionately, then left abruptly. Hardly a
show of coolness, whatever else it might be called.

'Connall was very helpful to me when I received the sad
news about my great-aunt's illness,' she said smoothly.

After the meal it was obvious that the two girls were ill
at ease in each other's company, and after a while Averil
excused herself, 'I need a breath of air.' She strolled around
the patio for a few minutes, noticing that a cover had been
thrown over the swinging hammock. Then on an impulse
she pulled the cover aside, sat on the long swinging seat.
The cover fell back of its own accord, but she was glad of a
short period of solitude. She needed to be alone to think out
all the implications of this new situation now that Renata
had apparently taken up residence in the villa. Averil could
not believe that it was more than a temporary whim, possibly sparked off by Connall in Averil's absence. She tried
to think of methods of inducing Renata to return to Cadiz,
but she guessed that a show of persecution would merely
serve to strengthen Renata's determination to stay.

Averil was on the point of going indoors when the hammock cover was gently pulled aside. 'Hallo, Renata!' said a
man's voice quietly.

Her first impulse was to spring up with an indignant
denial that she was Renata, but immediate second thoughts
persuaded her to stay.

'I'm sorry, Connall, to disappoint you,' she answered
softly. 'Shall I fetch Renata for you?'

'Don't bother. I can see her later. So you're back again
after your journey to England.'

'Obviously.'

'And your great-aunt?'

'She died soon after I arrived.'

'I'm sorry about that.' Even in the midst of her furious
annoyance, she heard the note of warm sincerity in his
voice.

'She left me the estate. So I've come back—to claim it.'
Now she bit the words off one by one. 'It was quite a sur-

140

prise to find Renata here—apparently under the impression that she could take possession. But of course you know all about that. The whole idea was probably your doing.'

'I? Good heavens, why should I do that?'

'You might have excellent reasons unknown to me,' she snapped.

'And I suppose you also had excellent reasons for dashing off to Seville with Don Rodrigo after I'd agreed to take you there for the plane.'

'Those reasons must be quite obvious to you, Connall. But don't let me waste any more of your precious time. You must be eager to talk to Renata and I don't want to spoil one of your nightly visits.'

She swung her feet to the ground and stood up away from the hammock.

'Nightly visits?' he echoed with a laugh in his throat. 'You make me sound like a nocturnal animal—like a bat or an owl.'

'Please yourself which animal you want to be.'

As she took a step away from him, he grasped her wrist and twisted her towards him.

'What's put you into such a temper?'

'I'm not in a temper,' she protested warmly, then controlled her tone again. 'But I'd like you to know, Connall, that I've come back here on business which I intend to carry out, however long it takes me. If you want to come to see Renata, please feel free to do so, but don't expect me to entertain you—in or out of hammocks!'

She wrenched her wrist free from out of his grasp before he could even begin to practise that soothing art of kissing her into a responsive mood. She was certainly not prepared to tolerate that again.

As she reached the covered part of the patio, she saw Renata reclining in a lounge chair outside the villa. A light from one of the rooms inside shone on her face.

'Your friend Connall is here, Renata,' Averil said brusquely as she walked past the Spanish girl and entered the house.

In the new room she had been allocated in her own house, Averil flung herself on the bed; she was shaking with

141

anger as never before in her life. So that was now the practice! The swinging hammock was exceedingly useful. With
the cover down to protect the upholstery from rain or dew,
the comfortable seat was an adequate haven for two in the
dark.

Connall had not seemed in the least abashed when he
discovered he had greeted the wrong girl. Useless to expect
otherwise, Averil told herself fiercely. He was no more than
a philanderer, generous with cheap kisses. Renata was welcome to him—until he tired of her, too, when the next
attractive girl came along.

After Averil had breakfasted next morning she sought
Gonzalo to explain her position to him, although she suspected that he had already been forewarned.

He greeted her with a cordial 'Buenos dias' and hoped
she had enjoyed her journey back to Spain.

She replied that she was glad to be here again at the
Serena and that as she was the new owner they must all
help to get the property into good shape.

With enthusiasm he told her about the new sets of tools
he had purchased for the men, hoes for the vines, cutting
knives for the melons, a new set of harness for the horses.

'This is the busy time of year,' he said. 'The summer is
short. Then the rains come again, so we have to hurry.'

'Yes, I understand. If there are further tools that you
need, please tell me and I'll try to get them for you. And
does my donkey Que Pasa? get a present?'

Gonzalo's dark leathery face crinkled into a wide grin.
'Que Pasa? has been waiting for you. Each day she looks to
find you. Go now and let her see you are back.'

Gonzalo went away to give orders to two of the men and
Averil reflected that his friendly air was a reward and a
relief. She had already wondered if Renata had poured
poison into the ears of Gonzalo and Marta, undermining
Averil's position in the household.

The donkey Que Pasa? made affectionate noises when
she saw Averil, who was charmed by the new red saddle-
cloth the animal was wearing.

'Come, Que Pasa?' said Averil. 'We'll go out for a ride
and see how our estate is faring.'

142

Even though she had been away for only a short time, Averil noted the great changes in the district during her absence. The sky was cloudless, the sun relentlessly drying up the waters; the young spring grass was already seeding and young birds, coots and terns, flapped about on the dry earth feeding on the fallen seeds. The lakes were smaller and consequently more crowded with the water birds. Averil was uncertain of the names of all the different kinds, but Connall would have known.

Angrily, she thrust the thought of Connall out of her mind. If she continued like this, she would soon regret returning to this countryside that held so many memories of him.

When she made a detour, she found her way blocked by the partly-made road that was to cut the Serena property in two. With a sudden pang of apprehension she prayed that Connall was not present at the point where workmen had told her she would find it easier for the donkey and herself. She had already dismounted, for she would not risk injury to Que Pasa?. She reflected that she could have been more careful in choosing her route this morning, but fortunately he was nowhere in sight and the men spread sacks across the rough stones and boulders that was to be the foundation of the road.

On her return to the villa Averil discovered that her old room had been restored with its former furniture and she wondered whom she had to thank for this gesture.

Renata was out somewhere, apparently in her car, and Averil mentioned the matter to Marta. 'Did you have the furniture replaced in my room?'

Marta's eyes shone with pleasure. '*Si, señorita*. I told the Señorita Bonaventa that it was your orders. You are the mistress here now.'

'Thank you, Marta,' Averil replied with gratitude. So the housekeeper was evidently on her side.

Renata did not return until early evening and then she seemed in her most amiable mood.

'You must come to Cadiz with me and visit my home,' she invited Averil.

'What will you do with it if you decide to stay here?'

143

asked Averil.

'Oh, one cannot have too many homes. It is a good thing. Here, the one in the country. In Cadiz, the one by the sea. There are good beaches, you understand, and much enjoyment in the summer.'

'I'll decide later,' said Averil coolly. 'I'm not sure exactly what my plans are for the next few days.'

It was then that Don Rodrigo's car drove into the patio. He greeted Averil with warm effusiveness, full of regrets that he had been prevented from calling sooner. 'As soon as I heard you had returned, I was overjoyed, but you should have let me know of your arrival and I would have met you in Madrid, and saved you the flight from there to Seville and the long journey here.'

'I wasn't sure myself,' she told him.

Renata had discreetly vanished after an initial greeting to Don Rodrigo, and now he sat close to Averil, holding her hand as though reluctant to let her escape ever again.

She told him briefly of the events in England and the fact that she was now the inheritor of the estate.

'Subject, that is, to the claims of Renata—and any others who think they are entitled.'

Don Rodrigo waved aside such obstacles. 'I shall personally make sure that there is no difficulty. My own lawyer will talk to your notary and settle the matter most successfully, I assure you.'

'Thank you,' she murmured, already a little uncomfortable at the idea of receiving further assistance from him.

'Now we must talk of ourselves,' he whispered. 'Oh, I have missed you. My life has been dreary beyond belief without you. You must not go away again. If you will consent, I should like to take you to Madrid to visit my family. Also, you ought to see something of our capital. You have not been there yet?'

'Not yet,' she admitted. 'But of course I had intended to go.'

Don Rodrigo smiled. 'It will be my pleasure to take you, show you the treasures of the art galleries, the life of the streets, the theatres, everything.'

Averil longed to find some way of damping down some

of his enthusiasm without actually insulting him. 'Will you stay to dinner?' she asked, as a means of deflecting him from his long-term projects in store for her.

During the meal Don Rodrigo gallantly divided his attention between the two girls, but Averil was keenly on the look-out for any signs that he might transfer his allegiance to the Spanish girl.

Renata, however, knew how to play a cool hand. Never a glance or a phrase that could be construed into anything but the friendly behaviour towards a dinner companion.

At the end of the meal when the three sat out on the patio with wine before them and Don Rodrigo scenting the air with his favourite cigar, he said to Averil, 'You should not be forced to live in this house, which is most unworthy of you. It needs so much to be done.'

'Which I intend to do,' she put in quickly.

'Oh, but I intend also to buy much new furniture and have the rooms decorated,' broke in Renata. 'That will be for me to decide.'

Don Rodrigo laughed. 'I must not be asked to play King Solomon. The matter will be settled in due course.'

Averil sensed that Renata was annoyed or disappointed by Don Rodrigo's impartial reply, for almost immediately she pushed back her chair with a harsh, grating sound intended to convey impatience. 'I will leave you both to talk, for no doubt you have much to say to each other,' Renata said coolly. 'Perhaps, Don Rodrigo, I shall see you tomorrow when I am out riding?'

In the dim light Averil smiled at this effort on Renata's part to annex Don Rodrigo, who had risen to bid Renata goodnight. In some ways, Averil would have preferred Renata to stay, instead of leaving her alone with Don Rodrigo.

But for the moment he began to talk of business matters, repeating his offer of the small triangle of land belonging to him, but now cut off by the new road.

'Now that you are the new owner,' he said, 'I can make my offer most definite. Also, there is another plan I would like to put before you, but you must not decide in a hurry. Think everything over well before you decide.'

'Yes?' prompted Averil, when he had made a lengthy pause. She wondered with some apprehension what else he had in mind.

'It is this.' He leaned his elbows on the small table in front of him and the light from the swinging lantern at the corner of the patio caught the angles and planes of his handsome face. 'If you found that this estate was too much for you to manage—you know that it has been very neglected, the house, too, is almost in ruins—it all needs a great deal of money spent on it to make it prosperous. I do not know if you have resources, or whether your family could advance you money for such needs—but you are in a difficult position.'

Averil glanced at Don Rodrigo. These broken, almost incoherent phrases were unlike his usual direct and concise speech. What was the project that was obviously making him so nervous? No, not nervous, that was unimaginable, but at least diffident about saying directly what was in his mind.

'Exactly what are you trying to say?' she asked gently.

'That I would most willingly buy the whole estate from you and give you a fair price.'

Although she had suspected the trend of his words, the actual offer fell on her ears like a stone in a pool. She remained silent for so long that he said, 'Come, Averil, you must say whether my offer pleases you or not.'

'I can't at this moment. As you said earlier, I couldn't decide in a hurry. I must have time to think.'

'If you like, you can consult your lawyer in Madrid and let him advise you.'

'Possibly I shall do that,' she agreed.

'But please do not speak of it to the Englishman,' he put in quickly.

'It's unlikely that I shall discuss my affairs with him,' she replied. But that was a give-away, for he grasped her hand and fondled her fingers.

'I am most pleased to hear that you do not confide in him. He is not to be trusted. You can see that already he is soon attracted to Renata. A fresh face is all he desires. When he goes to work somewhere else, then a new and

146

pretty face will make him forget.'

Averil merely smiled. It would never do to convey to Don Rodrigo that any possibility of a romance between her and Connall could ever happen.

When he left later in the evening, he had extracted a promise from her that she would come the following evening to dine at his house.

'Then we shall be able to discuss our future plans for Madrid—and after,' he suggested. That phrase 'and after' disconcerted Averil more than she cared for. She did not want to find herself tangled in a maze of half-promises that were construed into definite undertakings.

'Shall we spend the day at Cadiz?' invited Renata early the following morning.

'I thought you wanted to ride with Don Rodrigo,' observed Averil.

Renata waved away the handsome Spaniard. 'Oh, that will be for any time I like. Will you come in my car?'

Averil hesitated. 'I promised to dine at Don Rodrigo's house this evening. We'll be back in time?'

'Naturally, since I also am invited.'

'Good. Then we both have reasons for avoiding delay,' said Averil briskly, although it was a surprise that Renata would accompany her to Don Rodrigo's. Perhaps he was maintaining his role of impartiality.

'I will show you my house,' promised Renata as she drove along the main road and then through Jerez. 'But we do not want to spend the day sitting indoors. You have brought your swimsuit?'

Averil laughed. 'Of course. You said there were good beaches.'

The Bonaventa house was not large, but a delightful style of architecture with a small patio garlanded with flowers and climbing plants.

'You understand,' explained Renata, 'that in Cadiz in the old days there was not much space for building, so no one was allowed to build large houses or extensive patios. Now, people go out to the coast and build their new houses.'

'I like this very much,' commented Averil. 'Do you live alone here—when you're here and not at the Serena?'

Renata was amused at Averil's gentle jibe. 'I have two servants, of course. My mother died a few years ago, now I am in charge of my house.'

After a light lunch served out of doors in the patio, Renata suggested a stroll down to one of the beaches.

'You see that Cadiz is really not one town, but several small ones, like little islands joined together.'

Averil had previously examined a map of the coastal district, but now she saw the island towns linked by a ridge of sand and rock. It was easy to see why in its long history, Cadiz had been such a famous port, for its huge harbour afforded shelter and defence.

The beach to which Renata took Averil was windy and the fine sand penetrated everywhere. 'You will not notice the sand when we swim,' Renata assured her.

After her swim, Renata stretched herself out on a large towel and composed herself for a laze. For a short time, Averil followed suit, but eventually gave several anxious glances at her watch.

'Should we go back soon?' she asked tentatively.

'Plenty of time,' replied Renata sleepily. 'Do not fuss.'

Another half hour went by and Averil became impatient. 'Please, Renata, let us go back or we shall be late in arriving at Don Rodrigo's.'

With reluctance, it seemed, Renata obeyed, but when the two girls reached her house, she suggested that they both needed showers to rinse the sand from their bodies.

'All right, but let's be quick about it,' murmured Averil, taking her turn first.

When she was dressed again, she strolled out to the balcony of the first floor of the house and gazed at the beautiful turquoise sea ahead, deepening now towards sunset. She knew that this coast was called the Costa de la Luz—the Coast of Light—and the honey-gold shore was one of the most lovely parts of Spain she had seen. She would visit Cadiz again when there was more time to wander around the avenues and loiter in the plazas and she would prefer to be alone and not in Renata's company.

Now she was getting even more anxious over Renata's dilatoriness. At last the Spanish girl appeared, clad in a tawny brown satin sheath that flattered her dark hair and eyes and gave a rich glow to her olive skin.

'I am ready,' she announced. 'Come, we must go.'

As though Averil had not been waiting impatiently for the last hour!

But now there were further delays ahead. In the small side street where Renata's car was parked, two other cars hemmed her in.

'Wait, please,' she said to Averil, 'and I will get one of them moved.'

She disappeared round the corner. After some twenty minutes Averil alighted and looked up and down the street in case one of the other owners might be coming. She was quite certain now that Renata was deliberately engineering all these delays in order to prevent Averil from arriving at Don Rodrigo's by a reasonable time.

Another car drove slowly down the street, stopped at the end, and Averil took a few steps towards it, wondering if the driver might help to move one of the obstructing cars. But in the instant when he alighted, she saw to her dismay that it was Connall. Without hesitation she dashed back to Renata's car, bundled herself in and slammed the door. But Connall had already seen and recognised her. He stood outside the window and gave her a polite *'Buenas tardes'* which she did not answer, but stared stonily in front of her.

'I didn't expect to see you here, but of course it's a pleasure,' he continued.

No, she thought, you didn't expect to be seen arriving close to Renata's house. He was wearing fawn trousers with a linen jacket and cream silk shirt, so obviously he was dressed for calling on Renata, and this was no casual arrangement. Then Renata appeared, accompanied by an elderly man who apologised profusely for bad parking, entered his own car and drove off, leaving Renata clear.

She smiled at Connall and greeted him with enthusiasm. Then she adopted an apologetic air. 'You will forgive me, but I am forced to drive Averil back to her home, for she is most anxious to dine tonight with Don Rodrigo.'

'Oh, I see,' commented Connall. 'Then I mustn't detain

you both.'

'But no, it is not so simple,' protested Renata. 'We have been delayed and it is now late and perhaps we can make better arrangements. Now that you are here, we must all have dinner together here.'

'Not in the least,' snapped Connall, more to Averil than to Renata. 'I should not like to deprive Don Rodrigo of Averil's company.'

Now Averil spoke for the first time while this reshuffling was going on. 'I understood, Renata, that you were also invited tonight to Don Rodrigo's. Did you say that only to fool me?'

'I have changed my mind,' answered Renata. 'Don Rodrigo will ask you to dinner other times. Sometimes he will ask me, perhaps, but not always both of us together.'

'Then please decide now whether you want to drive me home or not,' said Averil firmly. 'If you don't, I'll get a taxi or hire a car to take me back.'

Renata shrugged and Averil saw the glance of resignation that she threw to Connall. 'It is most unfortunate, but——' She murmured a few words to Connall that Averil could not catch, then the last sentence was clear. 'I shall be back at the earliest moment and then we shall have the evening together.'

Renata seated herself at the wheel and pressed the self-starter. After a few attempts, it was clear that there was something wrong now with the car.

Averil alighted. 'You need not bother to explain, Renata,' she said. 'I can see now that this is all a put-up job, although I can't see your particular reason for preventing my return. You could have spent the whole day as well as the evening with Connall, if that was what you wanted. Why drag me into a day in Cadiz?'

'But, Averil, I assure you—it is only bad luck that has delayed us. I would have been back in time.'

'And bad luck that you dallied and delayed all the afternoon and evening, taking ages to dress yourself? I hope Connall appreciates all the trouble you've taken to make yourself attractive tonight.'

Connall was leaning against the wall of the house out-

150

side which the car had been parked. Averil became even more furious when she saw how much he was enjoying this scene between herself and Renata. If he had any decency, she thought angrily, he'd offer to drive me back, but of course that would be too much to ask. He would be deprived of Renata's company for more than a couple of hours. In any case, if he offered, she could scarcely accept, and she would certainly not beg him to help her.

Connall now began to examine the car, lifted the bonnet and poked about, muttering occasionally. 'Can't see anything obviously wrong,' he said eventually. 'Try the starter again.'

But the car would not budge.

'Then in that case I'd better make my own arrangements,' Averil declared. 'I'll find a conveyance of some sort.'

'But you must telephone Don Rodrigo first,' pointed out Renata, 'that you are delayed and will not arrive until later.'

Averil paused. It was nearly eight o'clock and practically dark. True, Spanish dinners did not start early, but she was far from home and from Don Rodrigo's house.

She accepted Renata's suggestion and went into the hall, but Don Rodrigo was apparently not available and Averil left a message with one of the maids.

'He will not expect you now,' remarked Renata, 'so you had better have dinner with us, Connall and me. Then we will find something to take you home.'

'Thank you, Renata. I prefer to eat in a restaurant—if I have any appetite at all. I hope you'll enjoy your dinner—with Connall.' Averil marched out of the front door, her head held high. Whatever happened to her, she would find her own way home.

Since this was her first visit to Cadiz, she was not familiar with the streets, but soon found one of the main avenues where there were several restaurants and cafés. Outside a shop window she paused for a few moments, asking herself whether after all the upset with Renata, she needed a meal. Might it not be better to try to hire a car somewhere? Then she reflected that today, merely for a trip to Cadiz, she had brought no great amount of money. There would be the double journey to pay for, to the Villa Serena and return, and she had little idea of how much that would cost.

On the other hand, she had eaten nothing since a light lunch and, hungry or not, she thought it wiser to treat herself to a snack. She found a large hotel with an adjacent snack bar and she chose a stool at the counter. While she was still reading the varied menu printed in large letters at the back of the counter, someone occupied the stool next to her.

An instinctive awareness of a particular presence caused her to turn her head. 'Connall!' she exclaimed, although her heart had already forewarned her of his identity. 'You needn't have followed me. I'm quite capable of taking care of myself.'

'Glad to hear it,' he answered laconically, and ordered some food for himself.

'Also you needn't have deprived yourself of the pleasure of dining with Renata,' she added.

'I suppose I'm allowed to decide that for myself? In any case, if she tricked you, she deserves to eat her meal by herself.'

A great surge of hope welled up within her. Could it be that he had followed her because he preferred a meal with her in a snack bar to an elaborate dinner with Renata? She could not dare to hope for such a possibility and quenched that rising elation.

When her plate of *canelloni* was served, she concentrated on eating.

'How sad,' he observed a few moments later, 'to think of two lonely people without the company they expected to sit at their tables! Dear Renata munching alone and Don Rodrigo with only his aunt, Doña Isabella, to keep him amused.'

Averil made no reply.

'You wanted me to drive you back straightaway when Renata's car wouldn't move, didn't you?' he pursued.

'It would have been a gallant gesture, of course,' she replied smoothly, 'but not one that I expected from you.'

'I was damned if I'd drive you to keep a date with the

152

handsome Don.'

Once again that heady elation took charge of her, but she did her best to quell this wayward sensation. Only a foolish girl would trust Connall or try to rely on the words he said or the tone of his voice.

'By the time you came it was too late anyway,' she told him. 'Renata frittered away as much time as possible.'

'Don Rodrigo should feel most flattered that you were so anxious to join him.' He cast her an oblique glance.

'I agree, and it was discourteous not to arrive.'

'True, true, so now you're not in such a hurry, we can take our time. The night is yet young.'

'But I have to return to Serena,' she objected. 'Perhaps you can tell me where I can find a garage that will hire a car.' Even as she said the words her inner hopes were prompting her to expect his reassurance that there was no need for a hired car.

'Oh, I can tell you that, but whether you will succeed at this time of night, I don't know.'

She stirred her coffee and did not look at him.

'Of course, I could offer to drive you myself,' he went on, 'but you're in such a petulant mood that I'm not sure that I want you for a passenger.'

'I'm not in a petulant mood,' she contradicted in a low, furious voice. 'If you don't want to take me, say so.'

He laughed. 'I had a sample of your waywardness that day I took you to Sanlucar—hopping off in a horse-carriage and giving me the slip, if you could.'

She waited in silence, then drank her coffee. Almost immediately he ordered more coffee for them both. Evidently he was determined to spin out the time and she was willing to enjoy his company. If only she knew how much was mere baiting on his part or whether he had any really deep feeling for her!

She discovered when at last they left the snack bar that his car was still parked in the street near Renata's house. So he had followed her on foot and she was overjoyed.

But in the car journey home, he seemed cold and aloof. She made one or two harmless remarks about nothing in particular and he answered abruptly or not at all. She sub-

153

sided into silence, but now although she was as close to him as she had been in the snack-bar, she felt that he had drifted many miles away from her.

By the time Connall drove to the Villa Serena it was past eleven o'clock. 'Have you to drive back to Cadiz?' she asked him.

'Is it any business of yours where I spend my nights? If I choose to drive around the countryside in the middle of the night, I suppose I'm at liberty to do so?'

Averil was choked at his rebuff, thanked him quietly for the drive home and said, '*Buenas noches.*'

He had halted outside the gates of the patio, as though unwilling to drive her right up to the villa, and she hurried across the patio as his car drove away.

Indoors, Averil asked Marta, 'Were there any messages? From Don Rodrigo?'

Marta nodded. 'Don Rodrigo was here at eight o'clock. He waited for you, then went away.'

'Thank you, Marta.' Eight o'clock. That was probably when Averil had been telephoning from Renata's house. Well, he would receive her apology when he returned to his own villa.

Taken altogether, the day had been an upsetting one, yet at the end of it Averil hardly knew whether to be sorry or glad. She was now wide awake and not at all sleepy. She went out to her small balcony and sat for a while, watching the faint shadows caused by a misty moon creep across the patio.

She could not fathom Connall's attitude. He had apparently been an expected guest at Renata's house that evening, yet he had deserted her to follow Averil through the streets and eventually drive her home. His abrupt changes of mood from gentle raillery to an icy composure disconcerted her. Yet nothing that he did or failed to do could force her to tear him out of her heart. She was landed with this aching longing for a man who prided himself on his ability to escape like quicksilver from any lasting association with any woman.

CHAPTER NINE

EARLY the following morning Averil saddled her little donkey and rode up to Don Rodrigo's villa. She must apologise in person for yesterday's failure and so far she could not telephone him, although, ironically enough, this morning engineers had arrived to re-install the telephone at Villa Serena.

Don Rodrigo received her slightly coolly, she thought.

'You realise that I would not have spent the day going to Cadiz with Renata if she had not assured me that she was also invited and therefore had to return early.' Even in her own ears Averil's excuses sounded lame.

'But I did not invite Renata, although if she had arrived with you—through perhaps some misunderstanding—then I would have welcomed her. But when I called at your villa last night and realised you had not yet arrived home, I was at first alarmed in case some accident had happened.'

'I should probably have telephoned a second time. Then you would have received my message direct.'

'But you are riding only a donkey this morning.' He changed the subject abruptly. 'You must have one of my horses, the one you had on other occasions.'

'But Que Pasa? must not be abandoned,' she objected. 'She likes me to ride her.'

Don Rodrigo smiled. 'She will be well looked after here, I assure you. Come and ride with me this morning.'

Averil felt it would be too difficult to raise too many protests, so she gave in, trying not to look at the donkey's mournful face and dejected head as she rode alongside Don Rodrigo from the stables.

When they were some distance from his villa and out on the fringes of his own estate, he said, 'Did Renata drive you home after all last night?'

Averil hesitated. There was no point in telling lies. 'No. She preferred to stay in Cadiz.'

'Then how did you come?'

She could probably have said, 'By hired car,' but she suspected that he already knew the identity of her driver.

'Connall brought me.'

He sighed deeply. 'I wish that Englishman would go away and lose himself in the high sierras. He is always at hand when he is least wanted.'

Not by me, thought Averil swiftly, but curbed such unruly ideas floating through her mind. 'He was calling on Renata,' she explained, 'and was probably staying to dinner with her, but when he saw that I was in difficulty, he offered to help me.'

That in itself was hardly true, but the best that Averil could manage, if Don Rodrigo would be satisfied.

'If I had known where you were, I would gladly have driven to Cadiz to fetch you,' he said slowly.

As they came nearer to one of the main roads, Averil noticed several horse-drawn cabs moving slowly south. 'Where are they going?' she asked.

'Home. They've been at the horse-fair in Seville for the past week. Now it is over and they go home.'

She remembered with a pang that Connall had promised to take her to the *feria*, but one way and another, partly through being away in England, she had missed the chance.

As she and Don Rodrigo reined in their horses to allow a splendid carriage pulled by a pair of grey horses to pass, she noticed that not only a woman and several children were fast asleep, but also the driver, a boy of no more than perhaps twelve years.

'But isn't that rather dangerous?' she asked, as other cabs came ambling behind them.

Don Rodrigo smiled. 'Not really. The horses will know every inch of the way, and in some cases, you see, the fathers of the families have already gone to their homes, possibly by bus or other means, so that they can work at whatever jobs they have. The horse-fair is very profitable for the cab-drivers. They make plenty of money in Seville, for the city is crowded with strangers and tourists for the whole week of the fair.'

When the two riders had crossed the road and taken another smaller lane, Don Rodrigo said, 'Next year you must let me take you to the *feria*. Since it is only an annual *fiesta* I must wait until then.'

'Perhaps we should not make promises for so far ahead,' she murmured. 'Much can happen in between.'

'Much indeed, and my first immediate hope is that you will now come soon to visit my family in Madrid.'

He talked at length of the welcome she would receive, of the sights of Madrid that would be a pleasure in themselves and doubly so in her company. In her mind Averil was trying to weigh the pros and cons of such an invitation. If she refused, Don Rodrigo would continue to renew his request until she yielded. If, however, she accompanied him, stayed with his family and found that she was not quite as welcome as he claimed, some lasting good might come out of the visit. If his family wanted him to marry someone else, they might put more pressure on him if they became acquainted with the English interloper.

Almost to her own surprise, she consented to accompany him the following week.

'How long shall I be away?' she queried.

'That is entirely for you to say. My family will be glad for you to stay many weeks, so that they can know you—and love you as much as I do.'

'Then I should not want this first visit to be longer than about a week or ten days,' she said firmly. 'You see, there is the property, which I must learn to look after and now Gonzalo and the men are working very well. So I can't neglect them.'

Don Rodrigo chose a path that would lead close to the Serena estate. 'This will be a short cut home for you.'

'Oh, no. My donkey is at your villa. I must fetch her.'

'Do not be afraid. One of my men will bring her.'

It dawned on Averil that Don Rodrigo's pride was slightly dented to be seen riding with a girl on a donkey and sheer perversity made her determined that she would go herself and collect Que Pasa?

'My little donkey is sad if I do not personally attend to her, so perhaps we can ride up to your villa and I will ride her home.'

He shrugged resignedly. 'As you wish,' he muttered briefly.

She had imagined that when they arrived at his stables, he would let her change mounts, but he directed her to continue riding the mare while the donkey was led on a rein.

When at last Averil patted Que Pasa?, attended to her feed and comforts, the girl began to laugh. 'Oh, my little *burro*!' she giggled, hiding her face against the donkey's head. 'The great Don doesn't like to be seen with you. You're much too humble.'

She remembered, though, that Connall had no such scruples. But she must turn her thoughts away from Connall and set her mind to preparations for the visit to Madrid. In one sense, this prospect caused her little uneasiness and she perceived that if she had really loved Don Rodrigo she would have been more apprehensive about her reception. She would have wanted his family to like her on sight, to welcome her into their intimate circle.

When Renata returned from Cadiz a couple of days later, neither girl made any reference to Connall or how Averil had made the journey back.

'I am going to Madrid next week,' Averil told the Spanish girl.

'To be introduced to Don Rodrigo's family?' Renata's eyebrows rose questioningly.

'Yes, and of course to do some sightseeing. I haven't seen Madrid yet, except the runway of the airport. I should like to know whether you intend to stay here or return to your home in Cadiz. I can then tell Marta how she is to arrange the household affairs.'

Renata began to laugh. 'Indeed! You are very much the mistress of the estate.'

'That point is not in dispute,' returned Averil smoothly. 'But I would be glad if you do not try to rearrange the bedrooms in my absence.'

'The changes I have made were improvements,' countered Renata.

'Possibly, but some changes should be made more gradually.'

Don Rodrigo lost no time in arranging Averil's visit to Madrid and in a couple of days she was driving with him to meet what might, in other circumstances, have been an ordeal.

His family house was in a quiet avenue near the Retiro Park. After the comparatively smaller Villa Serena, it seemed extremely spacious and luxuriously furnished. Some of the corridors were as wide as rooms, often decorated with carved wood panelling and oil paintings. There were several sitting rooms, ostensibly for various members of the family, so that they need not all gather in one place if they chose to be solitary.

Averil was presented to Don Rodrigo's mother, Doña Emilia, a small, round woman with black hair and gleaming dark eyes that would penetrate any undusted corners that maids might skip.

There was a guarded warmth about her welcome and Averil was glad that she had learned the correct polite phrases in Spanish for the occasion.

There were two sisters, younger than Don Rodrigo, Frasquita and Angelina, apart from two other relatives more or less contemporary with the mother. Averil supposed they were aunts. At dinner that evening further members of the family arrived, Don Rodrigo's two married sisters with their respective husbands and a cousin, Don Eduardo, with his wife.

Averil was glad that she had brought with her all the dresses and new outfits recently bought in England, for all the women of the Montilla family wore elegant dresses of satin or silk or printed nylon. Averil's dress of turquoise crêpe added an air of freshness and tonight she had pinned up her shoulder-length fair hair into an attractive swept-up style.

But of course she could not compete in the matter of jewellery, for as she glanced around the long oblong table she supposed that the combined value of the necklaces, rings and bracelets would be a small fortune. She had contented herself with a cameo pendant in mother of pearl on a slender silver chain. Apart from a gold watch and a few pieces of costume decoration, it was all the jewellery she possessed.

The dinner was protracted and elaborate with several dishes unfamiliar to Averil, but which she nevertheless tackled as though they were bread-and-butter, and she was grateful to Don Rodrigo for an occasional whispered explanation of ingredients. Her partner on the other side was a young man with a very high forehead, a small pointed beard and a Spanish accent which she found difficult to follow. After a few attempts to converse with her, he evidently gave up the struggle and turned to his own partner, no doubt with a sigh of relief that he had done his duty by the English miss who did not understand plain Spanish.

After dinner the party collected in what was apparently the largest drawing-room. Perhaps, thought Averil, it should properly be called a salon, for it was spacious enough to have accommodated fifty or sixty people in comfort. At one end was a full-sized grand piano, but no one was apparently in the mood to play.

The walls were covered with tapestries, but not the kind of classical or allegorical scenes that Averil had seen elsewhere in stately homes or museums. These pictures were of places in Spain, castles or fortresses, mountain scenes or village streets, all carried out in warm, glowing colours contrasting well with the dark wood wainscoting.

It now dawned on Averil that among the younger women was one Señorita Fernanda, accompanied by her father, and now this girl with beautiful Spanish features and a cloud of dark hair was deep in conversation with Don Rodrigo, while Averil was more or less chained to the side of his mother, Doña Emilia.

Was the girl Fernanda possibly the intended bride for Don Rodrigo? No doubt she and her father had been specially invited tonight to meet the English interloper who might have captivated Don Rodrigo. Even while she dutifully answered Doña Emilia's questions, Averil's glance strayed frequently to the girl, against whom she could feel no jealousy at all.

During Averil's stay in Madrid, there were several large dinner parties, occasionally a few guests to lunch, and the days were occupied by sightseeing. She was taken to the Prado to view some of the finest pictures in the world, the Goyas, the Titians, the great salon full of Velasquez, the Murillos.

'I should have to come here many times to appreciate, even to *see*, many of the paintings,' Averil said as she and Don Rodrigo paused before a magnificent portrait of the Princess Margarita who married the Emperor of Austria, and died tragically young.

'When we are married, you will be able to come as many times as you like,' Don Rodrigo whispered quietly close to her ear, and she realised that in her heartfelt enthusiasm for Velasquez' art, she had spoken carelessly. She must try to curb her tongue, for eventually he would not be to blame if he believed that she would be ready to join her life to his.

In the Royal Palace she was dazzled by the display of gold ornaments, a collection of superb workmanship, but she was also interested in the fact that the Palace stood on the edge of an escarpment from which could be seen a wide landscape stretching into the distance many miles away.

'We are high here,' Don Rodrigo told her, 'and the surrounding countryside is flatter. In the winter it is quite cold, so you must be prepared for even a little snow.'

Once again, that future tense caused Averil some uneasiness, and each time she tried to change the subject into some more harmless direction.

One of her favourite spots in Madrid was the Plaza Mayor, a large square off the main streets leading from the Puerta del Sol. Many of the surrounding buildings still had ornate balconies, and she learned that spectacular events had often taken place in the centre, so that they could be watched from the houses around.

Now there was only a centre monument in the midst of the cobbled square; several attractive cafés with outside enclosures afforded a place from which to view passers-by and the occasional car which raced diagonally through the corner arches.

'How odd,' she exclaimed to Don Rodrigo one day, 'that there should be so many hat shops around the square, most of them selling hats for men. Don't the men in Madrid buy their hats anywhere else?'

He laughed. 'It is perhaps a custom. I confess I had never thought about it.'

Then one evening near the end of her stay with the Montilla family, Averil saw the girl Señorita Fernanda in conversation with Don Rodrigo's mother, Doña Emilia. The older woman seemed to be comforting the girl whose face showed signs of anxiety. Later, after dinner, Fernanda seated herself beside Averil and for a few minutes talked of innocuous matters—sightseeing, the opera and so on.

Then she asked suddenly, 'When do you return to England?'

The question took Averil by surprise, but her answer was ready enough. 'I have no plans at all for return. I shall continue to live on the small estate I have inherited in the south. I want to make it prosperous and profitable.'

Fernanda's dark eyes opened wide in surprise. 'You will actually work on your estate?'

Averil smiled. 'Yes. Why not?'

Fernanda shuddered delicately. 'Oh, no. It would not be proper for you to act so if you were married to—to a Spaniard.'

Impulsively Averil laid her hand over the other girl's. 'But perhaps I have no intention of marrying a Spaniard.' As she said those words, she smiled with all honesty at Fernanda, who at length gave a slow smile in return. 'You understand?' added Averil.

The Spanish girl nodded and after a few moments rose to rejoin the younger Montilla girls. Averil reflected that at least she had done her best to bring comfort to the girl who evidently looked upon Don Rodrigo as her prospective husband. Whether Fernanda loved him, Averil had no means of knowing, but she wondered how long it would be before Don Rodrigo might learn indirectly of her reassurance to Fernanda.

On the day of departure, Averil was still cordially treated by Doña Emilia. 'I hope we shall see you again if you are visiting Madrid. You will always be welcome.'

The older woman moved to a small table where several packages elegantly wrapped had been placed.

'It is our custom to give small presents to visitors who come for the first time,' she explained. 'They are not valuable, but only a token for you to remember your visit. This is from myself and these from my daughters and my sisters-in-law. There is also one from Fernanda, who likes you very much.'

Doña Emilia selected a fairly large flat package with a label, 'From Fernanda'—followed by a string of family names.

'We also are very fond of Fernanda, for she is both charming and accomplished,' continued Doña Emilia in the most amiable tone.

Averil accepted the gifts in the most polite and gracious manner she could muster and once again thanked Providence that she was not in love and never would be in love with Don Rodrigo, or this exquisitely-staged dismissal would have broken her heart.

So with the collection of gifts piled in the car along with her suitcases, Averil accompanied Don Rodrigo back to the village on the edge of Las Marismas, and her own Villa Serena.

'You have enjoyed your visit to Madrid and to my family?' he asked just before he left her.

'Very much indeed, and thank you,' she said quietly.

'Then I may perhaps hope that now you will consent to the arrangements that I shall be happy to make.'

'Arrangements?' she echoed, knowing only too well what he meant.

'Arrangements for our betrothal and then our wedding.'

Averil hesitated. If she spoke plainly now and told him that she must refuse the honour of being his wife, he would merely take her in his arms and soothe her, tell her that she was tired by the sightseeing, meeting so many people, the journey home.

'I'm very tired, Don Rodrigo,' she murmured. 'Could we ride together tomorrow morning? Then we will talk.'

He was reluctant to go, but in the end she persuaded him, promising that she would be ready at eight o'clock.

In the privacy of her room, Averil knew that the visit to Madrid had in fact been a great success. If because of Connall's rejection of her or his perverse attitudes, his unwillingness to tie himself down, she had been even slightly swayed towards Don Rodrigo, then the last few days had cured her. She would have been suffocated in such an atmosphere of wealth and luxury, added to a strict code of behaviour as well as an even stricter attention to precedence both inside and outside the family circle. The decisions as to dinner partners, the rituals that attended so many aspects of gracious living among the Montillas, the careful selection of chaperones at various functions—all these outward manifestations seemed unimportant to Averil, no more than a 'pecking order' and perhaps they were only substitutes to cover otherwise empty lives.

While it was true that both the married daughters had children, there were innumerable maids to attend to those children's needs. Their mothers saw them or played with them only when the infants were washed and tidy, as little girls play with their dolls.

Don Rodrigo was waiting in the patio next morning when Averil went out to join him and mount the chestnut mare he had brought for her. Inwardly she smiled at the thought that he was taking no chances that she would come riding on a donkey to meet him.

For the first hour the two riders skirted the edge of the Serena property and Don Rodrigo commented on the condition of the fields and plantations. The vines were in better shape since the weeds had been properly cleared and the melons were reasonable, but needed better irrigation channels.

'Tell Gonzalo he should soon pay attention to planting out the rice,' he advised.

'I found it hard to believe that rice grew in Spain at all,' she commented, 'but now I've seen how wet this district can be, I'll believe anything!'

But chat about the land and its problems was only a preliminary to the real talk of the morning and Averil decided it would be better for her to open the subject.

'Don Rodrigo,' she began, 'this is very difficult for me, but I must tell you honestly that I can't marry you.'

He reined his horse to a standstill and she followed suit.

'Can I believe my ears?' he demanded. 'You really mean?'

She nodded. 'Yes, I do. Oh, I do appreciate the honour you have paid me in asking me, but I know that I'd never fit into your kind of life.'

'Because you have been to Madrid for one week and find my family strange? You must give yourself time to become accustomed to our ways. We are not monsters who will eat you or wicked people who will beat you.'

'I know that and all your family were most charming to me.' Averil could say that truly, for it was their cool charm without real warmth that had effectively warned her what would be expected of her.

He urged his horse forward and after a moment Averil followed. When she came abreast of him, he said, 'This is a great shock to me. I cannot speak or think clearly.'

'I'm very sorry, Don Rodrigo.' She fixed her glance between her horse's ears.

For some time the pair rode in silence until a clump of pine trees afforded shade and a place to tether the horses.

'Now,' he said, almost menacingly, as she dismounted. 'I must know the position quite clearly.'

'I've told you,' she persisted.

'But I love you so very much. How can you betray me like this?'

'I believe you love me—now, but it would not last. There is also the obstacle that I don't love you. I admire and respect you—but that's not love.'

He stared at Averil, unbelievingly, and now she felt pity for him, not so much because she was rejecting his love, but because he could not really believe that such an event would ever take place.

'Are you perhaps longing for the Englishman?' He shot the question at her as though to take her by surprise. If the relationship between her and Connall had been less clouded, she might have answered differently, but now she replied boldly, 'No, I'm not longing for the Englishman.'

That was an outrageous lie, for every fibre of her being longed every moment of the day for at least a harmonious friendship with Connall, if nothing more.

'Then if the Englishman means nothing to you, let me love you as only a Spaniard can.' Don Rodrigo pulled her into his arms with almost a rough movement and covered her face with kisses. She did not struggle, for that would have been absurd, but she remained passive and unresponsive. When he released her, he walked a few steps away and stood with his back to her.

Averil leaned against a tree trunk and waited until he turned suddenly, his face dark and scowling. 'You have ruined my life, my hopes!' he accused. 'I shall never find happiness now.'

He was behaving exaggeratedly, like a ham actor playing melodrama, but she knew that she must be tolerant to a Latin who was accustomed to highlighting his own heights and depths of emotion.

Without a word, he mounted his horse, leaving her to follow or not as she chose. Fortunately the little mare was not very tall and Averil hoisted herself into the saddle without difficulty. Don Rodrigo was waiting some distance along the road, where a fork led to one of the main roads.

'I see that it is hopeless to expect any other answer from you today,' he said. 'I realise I should not have rushed you last night with my talk of wedding arrangements.' He was much calmer now, even resigned. 'It was all too soon after your visit to Madrid.'

'It won't make any difference, Don Rodrigo,' she assured him.

He smiled at her. 'Time will make the difference. I will be patient and wait and I know that I can make you love me. Now we will not speak of the matter again for a few days.'

On arrival in the patio of her villa, he said, 'I have two requests to make and I hope you will agree. One is that I would like to give you the little mare you are riding, for your own use. She can be stabled here and you can ride her whenever you desire.'

'But I couldn't accept——' Averil began.

'Please, Averil. She knows you and she also knows the district. She will never lead you into danger. So please take her.'

Averil lowered her head and her colour rose. 'Thank you very much. What is her name?'

'Esperanza,' he answered. 'It means "hope".' After a moment, he added, 'My other request is that you come to the fiesta of El Rocio with me next week. It is something you should not miss, for it is held only once a year.'

She felt contrite that he had endured a frustrating morning and now she saw no harm in agreeing to accompany him.

When he had ridden away out of the patio, she led the mare to the stables, rubbed her down and fed and watered her. She must tell Gonzalo of the new addition to the Serena livestock. There were already four or five horses used for various purposes on the estate or for riding by the men. But Averil remembered to visit the little donkey Que Pasa? in her stall; that attractive little animal must not feel neglected.

Then Averil walked away from the stables and towards the house. For a moment she stopped dead in the middle of the patio and gazed critically at the ramshackle old place, parts of it still dilapidated. She was glad to be back, for now she knew she loved the *cortijo* and its faults. She would rescue the estate and the farmhouse from neglect and decay and perhaps hard work would help to ease the pain in her heart that Connall's unpredictable conduct caused.

CHAPTER TEN

AVERIL had temporarily forgotten about Renata, for she had not seen the Spanish girl since her own return from Madrid last night. So she was considerably surprised, as well as relieved, when Renata appeared at lunch and told Averil that she would be leaving to return to Cadiz.

'I do not really like this house,' Renata complained. 'It is almost falling down. It is most uncomfortable.'

'But what about your claim to the estate?' queried Averil with a smile.

Renata waved a beringed hand. 'Perhaps it is not so profitable after all. I see now what the lawyer said. That it would be a millstone around my neck. Much money needed to be spent and then where would the profit be?'

'I expect you're right,' agreed Averil amiably. 'So you're giving up any claim and will let me enjoy the place in peace?'

Renata laughed. 'Do you really believe you can find enjoyment here? Apart from Don Rodrigo, there are no other estates or farms near. There is no entertainment, no life, no gaiety. One would die of decay. I must have something better than that.'

Averil nodded. 'From your point of view, all you say is correct. I see the place differently.'

'You want to stay here because you think Connall will come back?' Renata's eyes glittered. 'He has now left this district and does not stay in his cottage.'

When Averil did not speak, Renata continued, 'You do not believe that? Then I could take you to the cottage and show you.'

'No doubt you have been to the cottage many times,' Averil said with disdain.

'Certainly,' agreed Renata with a sly grin. 'But he did not take you there?'

'There was no need,' snapped Averil.

Renata lapsed into silence. In the early evening she was

apparently ready to leave. Her car was piled with her belongings and she came to where Averil was sitting in the covered part of the patio.

'I go now. If you are in Cadiz at some time, then please call on me. You know I have a comfortable house there and am among my friends. I have not been happy here, because it is so miserable, but back in Cadiz, I shall blossom again like a flower.'

Averil wanted to say, 'Like deadly nightshade?' but bit back the unkind query. 'I wish you well,' she murmured.

Then, surprisingly, Renata sat opposite Averil. 'I have not heard much about your visit to Madrid. You have not told me about the family or all your exciting diversions.'

Averil laughed. 'Haven't you left it rather late to be asking these questions?'

'Of course not. I can drive home at any time. Tell me your impressions of Don Rodrigo's mother and other relatives.'

Averil sketched in lightly the numerous sisters and aunts and cousins.

'And now you are well received, so there is nothing to stop you from marrying Don Rodrigo. When does the wedding happen?'

'You're running ahead much too fast, Renata. We have not made any plans yet.'

'Oh, indeed? But you will be betrothed soon?'

'That, too, is not settled,' returned Averil guardedly.

'So slow. That is the English way,' sighed Renata. 'But let me give you advice. Do not let Don Rodrigo slip through your fingers because you think you are in love with Connall. He is not reliable, that Englishman, he flies from one girl to another. Look at the way he treated me when I took you to Cadiz! He walked out of my house when dinner was on the table. Where he went, I do not know, but I was left to eat alone—and I wept.'

'That was pretty well your own fault,' admonished Averil. 'You stalled and dallied—and in the end he was fed up with both of us.' Not for worlds would she admit that Connall had followed her and then driven her home.

Renata had a few more inquisitive questions to ask about

the Madrid visit, but Averil gave non-committal answers, and at last the Spanish girl said her goodbyes to Averil and Marta and the other maids and drove off.

Averil stared at the swinging hammock which Renata had left as a present. 'You will find it comfortable and useful,' she had remarked. 'In the daytime and also at night.'

Averil wondered if she would ever use it again, for it held the wrong kind of memories for her—the night Connall had apparently expected to meet Renata curled behind the covers; the night she had known Renata was there, because she had seen her foot protrude, but she could not be sure that Connall was also there.

No, the hammock could stay there for the summer. After that Averil would decide what to do with it.

There were other phrases Renata had used just before parting. 'I shall probably see you at El Rocio. Everyone goes there.'

For the next few days, Averil busied herself in the house. Marta wanted to know how the bedrooms were to be re-arranged now that Señorita Renata Bonaventa was not expected back.

'I think I might like to use the large room she had,' Averil answered. 'But you and Gonzalo could have one of the other much better ones than you now have.'

When she was supervising the rearranging of rooms and furniture, Averil asked Marta, 'How was it that so much stuff was piled in one of the rooms and the others left almost empty?'

Marta coloured under her dark, tanned skin. 'It was because the lawyer told us when Don Francisco died that there would be many people to claim all that was here. So we thought, Gonzalo and I, that we must keep a few pieces for ourselves, perhaps, or we would have nothing.'

'I see. You thought it was safer in your own room.'

'Si, señorita. Also, Don Rodrigo said he would buy some and give us the money.'

'And did he buy?'

'Only a table and some chairs. Nothing else—only the books.'

170

'The books?' queried Averil sharply. 'But I thought Gonzalo said they had been taken away to be valued.'

Marta smiled. 'No, he said that at first. But Don Rodrigo bought a lot of them. Some he did not want and he left those. They are still here in one of the rooms.'

Averil was thoughtful. Don Rodrigo had never admitted that he had bought some of the old man's books, although he had suggested that Don Francisco might have sold a quantity. She must remind herself to ask him when he took her to El Rocío for the pilgrimage.

Averil had already been warned by Marta and Ana, that quiet, elderly woman relative who moved about the corridors like a wraith when she was not stooping over the kitchen stove attending to saucepans.

'El Rocío is very noisy,' they told Averil. 'All night long. You will not sleep.'

'Oh, where do I sleep? Is there a hotel?'

Marta laughed. 'No, but cottages. Don Rodrigo has a cottage there.'

'And how long does this *fiesta* last?' Averil asked.

'Two nights, Saturday and Sunday. Monday, everyone comes home.'

'I see.'

So it was to be a week-end trip at Whitsun. Don Rodrigo had led Averil to believe that it was only a day's drive and then return. She consulted a map of the district and found that El Rocío was not only on the west side of Las Marismas, but impossible to reach from her side of the Guadalquivir, for there was no road or bridge that crossed.

On Saturday morning she telephoned, hoping that he had not yet set out, and asked how long she was expected to be away from home.

'Two nights,' he told her crisply. 'There is comfortable accommodation at my cottage in El Rocío. We use it only for this one week in the year.'

'Yes, I see,' she answered dubiously, and he must have heard that doubtfulness in her tone, for he added hastily, 'There will be others of my family there.' Then he laughed. 'We shall not be alone—I fear.'

Don Rodrigo had to make a long roundabout journey by

171

car, for he travelled some distance up the road to Seville before branching off to the west, then south again towards the coast but on narrow roads not designed for cars.

For the last twenty miles Don Rodrigo could do no more than move at a crawl, for the road was a solid jam of ox-carts gaily decorated and holding sometimes nearly a dozen passengers. Many of the men rode horses with girls in flounced polka-dotted skirts perched up behind. Hundreds of people in their gayest clothes mingled on foot between the cars, the carts and horses, and at every path or junction more people and vehicles joined the main procession.

'You see now why everyone comes on the Saturday before Pentecost,' murmured Don Rodrigo.

On the fringe of the small village he had to abandon his car and he and Averil walked up the thronged streets. It was a tiny village, Don Rodrigo told her, no more than eight or nine streets and usually deserted for most of the year.

The scene delighted Averil with its gaiety and colouring. Groups of eucalyptus trees gave protection and now beneath their shade refreshment stalls had been set up and women were busy setting out food of all kinds, men were arranging barrels and casks of beer on stands.

The cottage belonging to Don Rodrigo was decorated with garlands of flowers, paper chains and shawls, and Averil saw other houses decked up in a similar manner.

She was introduced to other women relatives of the Montilla family, two more cousins of middle age, but apparently Fernanda was not there and Averil was relieved on this account. So she thought, with an inward smile, she would be well chaperoned.

A small buffet meal had been set out in one of the downstairs rooms and Averil helped herself to some little patties and fruit, washed down with a glass of wine.

'You see we keep open house here during the next few days,' explained one of the cousins. 'Any of our friends are welcome to come and eat and drink whatever we have.'

Don Rodrigo suggested that Averil might like to go out into the streets where eventually the first parade would take place. 'But keep close beside me or you will be lost,' he warned her.

The noise was such as Averil had never before experienced. Flutes and guitars with drums and other instruments unknown to her created an excited clangour, gypsies sang and shouted, there was hand-clapping in the Andalusian manner, as in Seville, laughter and teasing, mock-fights.

But, apart from this boisterous din, there was one scene which Averil would remember for a long time. At the far end of a street, past the stone church, was a glorious wine-coloured sunset with golden streaks across the sky, reflecting a magenta glow on the distant sand dunes. The sun dipped beyond the horizon, the colours faded, leaving an iridescent sky of deep blue pricked with stars.

But it was now time for the parade to begin at the central plaza, the Real del Rocio, and the riders had lined up to pass by the chapel of the Virgin and pay their formal homage to the saint in whose honour this festival was organised.

When the parade was over, Don Rodrigo suggested, 'I think you would be wise to come indoors with me, Averil, for now the people become too excited and race through the streets most of the night.' He smiled at her. 'I doubt very much if you will get any sleep.'

Averil agreed to his suggestion and was interested in the numbers of friends and visitors who came in and out of the cottage, to eat perhaps a small item, drink a glass of wine and talk for a few minutes before visiting someone else.

On Sunday morning in the Plaza Real, a portable altar had been set up for Mass and riders attended, dismounting and kneeling when their turn came.

At night there was singing by innumerable groups of pilgrims and community brotherhoods, then bonfires and fireworks.

Don Rodrigo had told her that the Monday was the climax and Averil wondered if she could endure much further noise, although the whole *fiesta* was a spectacle that she would have been sorry to miss.

'One must be up early,' he said, 'to see anything. The procession starts about eight o'clock.'

Since her sleep had been punctuated by bursts of singing and shouting, with the accompaniment of drums and trum-

173

pets and a dozen other instruments, early rising was no problem.

She accompanied Don Rodrigo to a spot from which they would see the float carrying the Virgin. The statue bobbed about as though on a rough sea, for at almost every stage of the journey, men fought for the privilege of carrying the float.

By noon the Virgin was safely back in the chapel and the *fiesta* was virtually over. Don Rodrigo had said that he would drive home the next day if Averil agreed.

'There is so much traffic on the roads, so many horses and walkers, that it makes driving difficult.'

'Of course,' she agreed readily, and was glad to have the chance of watching the streams of people packing up and starting back to their homes. She wandered down one street and up another, deeming it fairly safe now that so many people had already left.

Suddenly she came face to face with Connall, leading his horse. She had not seen him since the night he had driven her home from Cadiz.

They greeted each other politely and Averil wondered if Renata were near at hand.

'So you came with Don Rodrigo, I assume?' he said.

She nodded. 'And you with Renata?'

'Good heavens, no! I came the opposite way round, from Sanlucar.'

'But that's on the other side of the river.'

He grinned. 'True, but our horses are ferried across in barges, then we go in small boats from a different point and wait for our horses. This is really the true pilgrim's way to come to El Rocio, not in a car. There are hundreds of horsemen from all the villages and towns around. Then we ride through the sand dunes. You could almost believe you were in the Sahara.'

'There was a most beautiful sunset here the night before last. That made me think of the desert.'

'Yes, I saw you looking at it.'

She turned her head sharply to look at him. 'So you knew I was here with Don Rodrigo.'

'When does the wedding take place?'

174

She could have told him the truth, but some demon of perversity made her ask, 'Have you the right to ask that question?'

He had drawn his horse slightly away from the throngs of people and carts and waggons. 'Yes, I think I have.' He looked away from her, then continued, 'You happen to be the only girl I've ever wanted to marry.'

His words fell on her ears like a startling blow and her heart was leaping about like a mad, trapped bird. But he was speaking again.

'... now that you've been to Madrid and met all his family, I can see how impossible it would be for you ... I've very little to offer and he can give you so much more ... so I won't trouble you any further. I'm leaving this part of Spain anyway for a job somewhere else ... I hope you'll be happy.'

He turned towards her and for an instant she thought she saw his eyes flicker with love, but the next moment he had mounted his horse. '*Adios!*' he called with a smile.

Her throat ached as she watched him ride down the street until he was lost in the crowd. She wanted to call to him, to run after him, to tell him the truth about Don Rodrigo, but somehow she was rooted to the spot and could only dumbly watch Connall riding out of her life.

She closed her eyes in sheer misery, then began to walk mechanically along the streets.

Someone took her arm and Don Rodrigo's voice sounded close to her ear. 'I thought you were lost,' he whispered.

Oh, yes, I am indeed lost, she thought bitterly.

'You should not have gone among the crowds alone,' he rebuked her, 'but now you are safe.'

Every word that he said echoed with a different meaning in her mind. Safe? Never again, for she would always be tortured by the vision of an enchanting happiness that she had thrown away for the sake of pride.

She felt as though she had been turned to stone, icy, frozen, with only an outward shell to cope with everyday realities concerning other people.

Eventually her unresponsive attitude penetrated Don Rodrigo's sensibilities. 'Something has happened. I saw the

175

Englishman a few moments ago and I think you have also seen him. Tell me, please, my love, what he has said that distresses you so much.'

She tried to smile. 'It's nothing. Nothing at all.'

He sighed. 'When I brought you here, I thought I might still persuade you to marry me.'

'No, Don Rodrigo, don't let us discuss all that again. My answer was really final.'

'But you would marry the Englishman if he asked you? Not that he could offer much! A man who is employed on roads and is ordered from place to place, even one country to another. He has no home, nothing.'

The fact that Don Rodrigo had elaborated on Connall's position gave her time to answer with some control. 'Oh, he is going to another part of Spain immediately, so I shall not see him again.'

Don Rodrigo smiled. 'That is good.'

'It makes no difference to us,' she asserted, for it was now or never that she must make her decision quite plain to him. Otherwise she might find herself caught up inevitably with Don Rodrigo. 'I do not intend to marry anyone for quite a long time,' she said now. 'I shall work on the estate and make it as flourishing as I can. I like Spain and I enjoy living here, but I'm not ready to marry anyone yet.'

When she paused he remained silent, and she continued, 'Please, Don Rodrigo, don't you see how impossible it would be for me? I don't love you, but Fernanda does, and she would make a much better wife than I.'

'But it is not Fernanda I want. It is you!' he declared.

'At the present time, yes. But you would soon realise that we're not suited. You would probably find me too independent because I am English.'

He gave her a steely glance. 'I am beginning to think so. You are too independent for a Spanish wife, so you would have to change.'

'Exactly,' she retorted, 'and I might not want to change my nature.'

He escorted her back to the cottage, but after a while she noticed that he was no longer among the various visitors and friends who had called. Probably he had gone to seek more dependable masculine company away from the contrariness of women.

When he drove her home next day she asked him point blank about the sale of Don Francisco's valuable books.

'Did you mean that you bought some from him? Or was it after he died?'

'Both,' he answered. 'He needed money, and after his death I bought others to help Gonzalo.'

She was reluctant to argue with him, but she had no idea whether he had paid a fair price, and in any case she was of the opinion that the books belonged to the estate and should not have been sold before the legal matters were settled.

She changed the subject. 'I think I must return Esperanza, the mare you gave me.'

He jerked his head towards her. 'No! That would distress me very much. Keep her—to remember me.'

A parting gift? Like those others from the Montillas in Madrid, she thought, the chocolates, perfume, the silk shawl and leather writing case.

A few days after her return from El Rocio, Averil received a note from Don Rodrigo, saying that he would be staying in Madrid for some time, but if she needed his help or changed her mind about marrying him, he would be glad to hear from her. His letter gave her the impression that in all the circumstances he was not too grieved to say goodbye to her.

By now the summer days were already baking hot, as Connall had informed her earlier. The many streams that criss-crossed the meadows had dried up and the carp floundered from one little pool to another, seeking their way to more permanent water until they perished on the dry earth. Then the kites and vultures would swoop down and clean up the dead fish.

There were now great flocks of herons scouring the dried earth for food; the young ducklings, however, did not fare so well, for they often padded about on their awkward feet trying to find water where now was only baked ground. Eventually they fell prey to numerous predators of the marshes, the lynx and the fox, the eagles and hawks.

Sometimes Averil sighed to think of the natural destruction that went on all over the meadows and marshes, but she realised that always the appropriate number of each species would survive.

She promised herself a visit to the Coto Doñana, the wildlife preserve some miles on the other side of the river and nearer the coast. This had now become internationally famous as the sanctuary of dozens of birds and animals which might otherwise become extinct.

But for the time being, she must give her attention to her own estate. One morning she was surprised and delighted to receive a letter from the notary in Seville, informing her that the compensation for the road had now come through and was a rather larger sum than could have been expected.

She told Gonzalo and Marta the good news. 'We'll drink a glass of wine together. Now we shall be able to afford many improvements. The house, the stables and barns, and the fields.'

When she re-read the notary's letter, the name of Señor Brunner sprang out of the paper. '... the evidence of Señor Connall Brunner at the court when you were not present ... cutting the Serena estate in two ...' she translated.

Averil stared into space with the letter in her hand. So Connall had gone at some time to represent her at whatever court decided the compensation. She had known nothing of such a meeting. Could it be that Don Rodrigo had known of the necessity of making an appearance, since he was also involved, but had failed to tell her?

She sighed with despair that she had so alienated Connall, yet surely there must be a tinge of hope somewhere. If she knew his address she would write and at least thank him.

She would not communicate with Renata in the matter, but cautiously she approached Vanna, Gonzalo's daughter, who might know the cottage where Connall had lodged in the village.

'He has gone a long time ago,' Vanna told Averil. 'If you wish, I will take you to the house and we will ask the *señora*.'

But the woman knew nothing of Connall's present ad-

178

dress. 'He said he was going to the mountains, but where I do not know.'

Averil thanked the woman and looked with interest at this small stone cottage where Connall had stayed.

A week or so later, Vanna told Averil, 'She says she thinks it was the Sierra Morena, that woman, where the English *señor* stayed.'

'Thank you, Vanna. It doesn't really matter,' replied Averil. The Sierra Morena stretched for about three hundred miles across the southern lands of Spain. It was like saying someone had gone to the region of the Alps.

For the next three months Averil busied herself with the affairs of the Serena estate, attending to the renovation of some of the more neglected parts of the house and helping Gonzalo with the practical matters of the fields, as well as keeping the accounts.

She had prevailed on Gonzalo to pay more attention to the marketing of the produce and now he had a small van to take melons and eventually figs and grapes to outlying villages as well as Seville. The results for this early part of the season were encouraging.

Absorbed in her new career as owner of a small estate in Spain, she postponed making any decision as to when she might return to England, although her parents frequently advised her to do so. She had thrust her unhappiness and loneliness to the more remote corners of her mind and was trying to forget she had ever known Connall.

Then one evening Gonzalo returned from Seville and was casually reading a newspaper, when Averil saw headlines about an explosion and landslide in the Sierra Morena.

Part of a new road being constructed had collapsed, she read, and several men had been killed or injured. Her fears were quite stupid, of course, for there would be several roads being constructed somewhere along the Sierra.

An hour later Renata telephoned from Cadiz. 'Do you know there has been an accident in the mountains near Cazalla? That was the place where Connall was working.'

Averil caught her breath with a gasp. 'I've heard about the accident, but I didn't know where Connall——' she broke off in embarrassment.

'Oh, then perhaps it doesn't matter for you. I expected you would be sorry in case he was hurt. I hope very much he is not involved.'

'I hope so, too,' returned Averil. 'Thank you, Renata, for letting me know.'

Renata prattled on for some minutes, informing Averil that she was shortly to be married to a wealthy Cadiz businessman. Averil was in a fever for the Spanish girl to finish, but forced herself to listen in case Renata had any further information about the place where Connall was working.

When at last she was able to replace the receiver, Averil went to Gonzalo. 'How far is this palace, Cazalla de la Sierra?' she asked.

He looked thoughtful. 'I do not know. Many kilometres, perhaps.'

'We must find it on the map.' She found a ragged old map in a drawer of her desk.

'It's here,' she pointed to the place. 'Will you take me in the van? The English *señor* may be hurt and I must go there.'

'But tonight?' he queried in dismay.

'Tonight. We will have a quick meal and set out.'

Marta was helpful when she saw that Averil was determined to leave as soon as possible, and while the latter and Gonzalo were eating, the housekeeper prepared a package of food and wine to take with them.

Gonzalo was not familiar with territory much beyond Seville. To him Cazalla was at the ends of the earth, beyond the mountains and therefore an unknown land. He took one wrong turn after passing through Seville, but Averil with the map on her knees directed him to continue and then take another road which would lead to Cazalla.

This turned out to be a mistake, for the road wound upwards through the mountains and Gonzalo had to drive slowly and carefully to avoid disaster.

By the time they reached Cazalla, it was deserted, for it was past three in the morning. There was no one to ask where the accident had occurred.

'We'll go to the Guardia Civil and ask,' decided Averil. The policemen shook their heads and advised against driving to the scene, which was some distance along a narrow road out of Cazalla.

'We must go,' declared Averil firmly.

Reluctantly the police gave her directions and with Gonzalo she set off again, but after about five or six miles they came to a road block beyond which traffic was not allowed.

Averil alighted from the car and asked for news. Various officials shook their heads and said they did not yet know what had really happened. When a police car came to the barrier, she asked if they would take her at least nearer to the scene. At first they refused, but when she told them that she was the fiancée of one of the men involved, they agreed.

It was a bold step to call herself anyone's fiancée, but she argued that in this case the end justified the means.

Even then, the police car could not proceed beyond a further barrier, but here there was a rough café of sorts and the proprietor had remained open throughout the night to serve refreshments to the rescue teams and other workers.

One of the Guardia Civil in the car volunteered to try to obtain information for her.

'What is the name of the man you are seeking?' he asked Averil.

'He is English. Connall Brunner.'

'A tourist?'

'Oh, no. He works on the roads.'

Even in the midst of her excruciating anxiety and distress, Averil smiled to herself at her description of Connall. She had made him sound like a road sweeper or a man who patched up worn places!

After some twenty minutes or so, the policeman returned. 'There is no news of an Englishman. Three Spanish workers are injured and have been taken to hospital. Rescuers are trying to find others who are missing.'

Averil thanked him and decided to wait inside the café. She took her coffee to a table by the door so that she could ask new arrivals if there were any fresh news. Eventually, she sat outside at one of the rough wooden tables from which vantage point she could see any vehicles that passed.

Once, the proprietor came out to ask if she needed more coffee. 'It is cold, *señorita*. The coffee will warm you.'

When he brought it and she took the first sip, she found that he had laced it generously with a good tot of brandy. Yet again she reflected on the innate charm and thoughtfulness of most of the Spanish people. Even Gonzalo and Marta had only appeared unfriendly at first because they dreaded an unknown intruder.

An ambulance drove slowly towards the road barrier and Averil ran towards it. When it stopped, she asked someone standing near if he knew who was in there.

'No one will tell us anything,' he grumbled in reply.

The ambulance drove off in the direction of Seville and Averil was left regretting that she had not boldly asked who was inside. Supposing among the patients was Connall, badly injured or—even worse? She refused to face the fact of death. If he were dead, then all the colour and music of her life had gone, the tune jangled, the colour faded and drab. Without Connall her life of loneliness stretched endlessly before her.

A second ambulance arrived and this time two men jumped out of the back. She ran towards one of them to ask for news, then realised that the other was—could it be Connall, this haggard-looking man, his face plastered with mud, his clothes torn and muddy?

'God in heaven!' he exclaimed. 'What are you doing here?'

The roughness of his greeting convinced her that the man was indeed Connall.

'I came—because of the accident—I had to know——' Her words came incoherently because she wanted to throw herself into his arms and weep as never before.

Somehow they were sitting at one of the wooden tables.

'You mean you came all this way to know if I were dead or alive?' he asked incredulously.

'Alive, for preference,' she retorted with some of her old spirit, for only that control would save her from bursting into tears.

'And Don Rodrigo allowed you to?'

'Don Rodrigo is in Madrid, probably asleep and not concerned with accidents in the Sierras. Gonzalo drove me here, but I had to leave him at another barrier down the

182

road. But you must get out of those wet clothes and I'll order you some coffee.'

She had half risen, but he grasped her wrist with his muddy hand. 'The coffee can wait. I want to know why you've come all this way.'

'I've told you. I wanted to know.'

'Know the worst? For what reason? So that you could go home with a clear conscience that I wasn't dying of a broken heart?'

She was tired from anxiety and the long drive through the night. She had come to prove her devotion and all he could do was jeer. She wrenched her hand out of his grasp and stood up.

'I'm sorry I wasted my time—and Gonzalo's time, too,' she broke out angrily.

Then she saw the look on his stained and drawn face and was immediately contrite. As he stood up she saw how weary he was, grasping the table for support.

'I'm sorry,' he said before she could speak. 'I'm so damn tired I don't know what I'm saying. It's only that I just can't believe it's true—you came because you thought I was in danger.'

'What else?'

'Nothing else?'

She sighed. 'Because—you provoking, cantankerous, cross-grained hulking brute—because I love you!'

The grin that slowly spread across his unshaven face delighted Averil more than any expression she had ever seen on any man's face before.

'Say it again, darling. I can't believe it the first time.'

'Why should I? When did you ever tell me that *you* loved me?'

'I wanted to marry you. Wasn't that enough?'

'No! Every girl wants to hear the right words.'

'I think I fell for you when I fished you out of an *ojo*. Remember?'

'I remember, and now I know what an *ojo* is. It's the hole in the marshes that you fall in.'

'There were times when I wished I'd passed by and not

rescued you, but I couldn't stop myself—and then I was lost.'

The dawn light was coming up over the eastern mountains and Averil recalled herself to practicalities. 'Come, Connall, you must have some coffee and food and dry clothes.'

She pulled him towards the café and he glanced down at her with that same light in his eyes which she thought she had seen at El Rocio and then dismissed as wishful thinking.

'Yes, the sooner I get cleaned up, the sooner I'll be able to kiss you in style. I can't touch you while I'm in this filthy state, but I've been down in the river helping to search for some of the men all day and all night.'

She persuaded him to drink a mug of coffee first before he left her. The café proprietor's wife was busy preparing hot baths for all the men who needed them, and that was almost everyone in the café, apart from the officials and the police.

When he rejoined Averil again in the bar, he was wearing borrowed trousers and a donkey jacket someone had lent him. 'I think we must have a small celebration,' he said, and ordered champagne, but the proprietor apologised that such wines not exactly being in his line, all he could offer was brandy or local wine.

'Then brandy it is, and you'll drink a toast with us.'

The man beamed and poured large goblets of potent brandy for all three.

'So early in the morning,' remarked Averil with a laugh. 'I'm not sure I can take such heady stuff.'

Then the policeman who had come in the car with her up to the barrier came across to the café and grinned at her.

'You have found your fiancé?' he queried. 'That is good.'

Averil coloured to the roots of her hair.

Connall put his arm around her, nodded to the Guardia Civil and whispered to Averil, 'Jumping the gun?'

'I had to tell them something or they wouldn't have brought me. I couldn't very well say I was someone's wife. They would have seen I had no ring.'

He lifted up her left hand. 'We'll remedy that omission

184

as soon as possible. But let's get away from this crowd. I've got a lot to say to you.'

It seemed that Connall had plenty of action in store for her, for outside the café, away from the cluster of cars and officials, he held her close to him and kissed her, as he had promised, 'in style'. It was a very satisfactory style, thought Averil.

'Oh, Averil my love, I don't want to part from you ever, but you must understand that I've so little to offer you and I lead a rough life, at least for the next few years. There'll be no settled, comfortable home, no luxuries.'

'It's the man that counts, not where he lives or what he has,' she told him, and put her arms around his neck and drew his face towards her own.

After a long interval, she said, 'I have a home here and we can both be happy in it. You'll see what improvements I've made—thanks to your help with the compensation money.'

'Oh, you've discovered that.' He looked a little shame-faced. 'I piled on the evidence in your favour because I knew Don Rodrigo wouldn't help you there.'

'He wanted to buy my estate.'

'Yes, he said so, but he wasn't really in earnest. If you'd married him, the whole lot would have become his property without spending a single peseta. But there again——' his face clouded, 'I'm not sure I can accept a home at the Serena. I can't marry a rich wife.'

She laughed and her laughter echoed on the early morning air. 'A rich wife! Why, we haven't finished paying off some of the debts yet. Be thankful, Connall Brunner, that I have a roof over my head when you go careering off into the mountains. Tell me what happened at the accident.'

'We were blasting sections of rock to widen the road where it goes above the river, and the explosion happened before it was due. Consequently, some of the men were too near and several of them were knocked over the edge down into the river.'

'Were there many hurt?'

'Four or five. None killed, fortunately, but we had to search a long time to find two men who were trapped under

185

boulders.'

'And you? Where were you when the blast happened?'

Connall smiled. 'At what I thought was a safe distance, but I took a toss into the side of the mountain and bounced off it. Only a few bruises and cuts.'

'Then we ought to get home as soon as possible. I've left poor Gonzalo waiting miles back with the van.'

Someone gave them both a lift back to the van and now Connall took the wheel for the drive home. 'I know the road very well,' he told Gonzalo, 'and you've put in a long day and night.'

On the way, they stopped once to picnic from the large parcel of food Marta had packed, so it was early afternoon when at last they arrived at the Serena estate.

'You must rest for a couple of hours,' Averil persuaded Connall. He agreed without argument and she guessed that he was to tired to dispute.

Towards dusk when Connall was refreshed, he and Averil went out and walked along part of the new road, where it was newly surfaced. They spoke of plans for their future.

'In the autumn I shall go back to England to see my parents,' she said.

'I shall come too. I'm not letting you that far out of my sight. I've a few things to do there myself. I have some leave due in October. Actually, I have what you might call something in the way of resources. I own a half-share in my brother's farm.'

'Oh, where?'

'In Gloucestershire. He likes farming, he's married and has two small sons, and while I rove about gashing the countryside with roads, we settle amicably about the profits.'

'So you see you're just as much a landed proprietor as I am!' she exclaimed with delight. After a pause, she said, 'My family will love to come here for holidays—so will yours, probably.'

They had come to a part of the estate from which they could view the wide expanse of Las Marismas and although the sunset glow was more pink than mauve, Averil felt the

186

peace of this strange, wide country tug at her like a magnet.

'Wait a few minutes here,' commanded Connall. 'When the pink fades, you get that amethyst colour.'

He was right and the lovely mauve iridescence shone over the distant horizon, then faded into night. Overhead the sky was already pricked with stars and a faint breeze sprang up to cool the long day's heat.

'We must go to the Coto Doñana,' he said, as they turned to walk back to the villa. 'I've wanted to take you there. There's a small palace right in the heart of the wildlife preserve. Sometimes I think I'll give up road-building and become a warden. Much more satisfying.'

She leaned towards him. 'I think you're really a farmer at heart. You like growing and preserving things, instead of what you call "road-gashing." So in due course, we'll make the Serena estate one of the most prosperous in Andalusia.'

'And when the rains come?' He gave her an oblique teasing glance. 'Will you grumble about the incessant wet?'

Averil laughed. 'I shall only say it's good for the melons and the rice, as well as the birds.'

By the time they reached the villa and entered the patio heavy dark clouds had piled up on the horizon. 'By the look of the sky the rainy season is not so far off,' Connall prophesied.

Averil's glance fell on the swinging hammock. 'There's one thing I want to know.' She fixed Connall with a steely glance. 'That night when you found me in the hammock instead of Renata, were you disappointed?'

He roared with laughter. 'I've been waiting to hear you demand that explanation.' He pulled her closer towards him. 'I knew you were there, but I pretended to expect Renata, hoping it would make you jealous.' He looked down at her face. 'And were you?'

'Madly jealous!' she admitted happily. 'I couldn't speak a civil word to you.'

'I know, but I went away almost happy because I'd succeeded in arousing even a little bit of jealousy. If you'd appeared completely indifferent, then I don't think I would ever have come here again.'

Suddenly great drops of rain plopped on the dry flagstones of the patio, on Averil's and Connall's heads, as they dashed for shelter to the covered part of the patio.

'This is where I came in,' said Averil. 'The rainy season is already here.'

'Oh, it comes punctually almost to the date, last week in September,' Connall replied. 'But autumn is a wonderful season here on the marshes. It takes a week or two to moisten the cracked, parched earth and even more to make the lakes join up together. Then the water birds come, millions of them. First a few ducks and geese from the northern parts of Europe, then in greater numbers. The dry river beds creep back into life, the lakes widen and all kinds of grasses and flowers appear, as though they're relishing a second spring.'

Something of the deep love that Connall felt for this part of a land foreign to his own communicated itself to Averil.

'One day I shall love Las Marismas as much as you do,' she said. 'We ought to thank my great-aunt Freda for sending me here—and perhaps far back in time dear Don Francisco.'

Connall pulled her closer towards him and kissed the tip of her nose, while heavy rain thundered on the roofs. 'We'll thank anyone who sent us to Las Marismas.'

'I call them the amethyst meadows,' she answered.

Golden Harlequin $1.95 per vol.
Each Volume Contains 3 Complete Harlequin Romances

☐ Volume 20

DOCTOR SARA COMES HOME by Elizabeth Houghton (#594)
After an unfortunate mishap, Sara Lloyd, a brilliant doctor went to live for a year in the delightful but remote Welsh Mountains. Coming to terms with life again, she found Robert Llewellyn becoming a very dear friend, then, suddenly, out of her "hidden" past walked — Stephen Grey.

THE TALL PINES by Celine Conway (#736)
Bret was deeply involved in chemical research in Western Canada. The last thing he needed on his mind was this pale, fragile English girl, and her foolishly quixotic mission. The "last thing" soon became the most important part of his whole life . . .

ACROSS THE COUNTER by Mary Burchell (#603)
Katherine was assigned to re-organize one of Kendales' departments in the Midlands. Within a week, she became engaged to Paul Kendale while she still loved someone else — it wasn't the shop, but her own life which underwent the greatest change . . .

☐ Volume 21

THE DOCTOR'S DAUGHTERS by Anne Weale (#716)
When the new squire arrived at Dr. Burney's busy and pleasant household, his presence became a disturbing influence on the lives of all the doctor's family. It was the eldest daughter, Rachel, who quickly found that Daniel Elliot was not a man to be ignored:

GATES OF DAWN by Susan Barrie (#792)
Richard Trenchard was accustomed to having his own way, not least with women. This applied even to his sister, and to her secretary, Melanie Brooks, who fell victim to Richard's power. But, in the end, was it Richard, or Melanie, who really did have their way?

THE GIRL AT SNOWY RIVER by Joyce Dingwell (#808)
Upon arrival in Australia, Prudence found herself the only girl among 400 men! To most women, this would have been heavenly. But, what if the most important of these men is determined to get rid of you — as was precisely the case . . .

Golden Harlequin $1.95 per vol.
Each Volume Contains 3 Complete Harlequin Romances

☐ Volume 25

DOCTOR MEMSAHIB by Juliet Shore   (#531)
Mark Travers had little use for a woman plastic surgeon in his hospital in Bengal, but the Rajah had requested her, so he might make use of her visit. An accusing, anonymous letter had preceded Ruth's arrival, and try as he did, Mark could not quite put it out of his head . . .

AND BE THY LOVE by Rose Burghley   (#617)
"Is it necessary to know all there is to know about a man or woman before falling in love with him or her?" When Caroline was asked this question, her answer came easily. It was later that she would have cause to weigh the value of these words . . .

BLACK CHARLES by Esther Wyndham   (#680)
A man who would never marry! Whose character was arrogant and fierce! He was the one dark haired male born of this generation into the Pendleton family, and alas, it was the fate of young Audrey Lawrence to cross swords with — Black Charles Pendleton.

☐ Volume 27

SANDFLOWER by Jane Arbor   (#576)
Both girls were named Elizabeth. Roger Yate thought Liz to be forceful and courageous, and Beth, sweet appealing little Beth. In his opinion of the characters of these two girls, the brilliant young doctor could not have been more wrong!

NURSE TRENT'S CHILDREN by Joyce Dingwell   (#626)
A tragic accident had ended Cathy's training, so she came to Australia as housemother to a number of orphaned children. Dr. Jeremy Malcolm seemed to take an immediate dislike to her organization, and more particularly, to Cathy herself.

INHERIT MY HEART by Mary Burchell   (#782)
The only way left for Mrs. Thurrock and her daughter Naomi to share the inheritance now, was for Naomi to marry Jerome. It might have been a good idea, if only Naomi hadn't infinitely preferred his brother, Martin . . .

Golden Harlequin $1.95 per vol.
Each Volume Contains 3 Complete Harlequin Romances

☐ ## Volume 31

THE HOUSE ON FLAMINGO CAY by Anne Weale (#743)
Angela Gordon was glamorous and ambitious, and confident that in the Bahamas she would find herself a rich husband. The wealthy Stephen Rand was perfect, but alas — he was much more attracted by her sister Sara's quieter charms . . .

THE WEDDING DRESS by Mary Burchell (#813)
Loraine could hardly contain herself, she was going from the seclusion of an English boarding school, straight into the heady atmosphere of Paris, in May. Her only concern was, her unknown guardian — and his plans for her . . .

TOWARDS THE SUN by Rosalind Brett (#693)
There was a warm loveliness all around her on the sun-soaked South Sea Island of Bali, yet, Sherlie was miserable. She was exploited by a chilly stepmother and even worse, she fell in love with the totally inaccessible — Paul Stewart.

☐ ## Volume 32

DOCTOR'S ASSISTANT by Celine Conway (#826)
Laurette decided that Charles Heron was an autocrat, who thought far too much of himself. She also knew that she meant absolutely nothing in his life — a suitable situation? Quite, — until she realized, that for the very first time, she was in love!

TENDER CONQUEST by Joyce Dingwell (#854)
Bridget found her work fascinating. She loved travelling around, meeting and talking to all sorts of people, who all seemed to enjoy talking to her. All, except the new Market Research Manager, who considered her quite inefficient.

WHEN YOU HAVE FOUND ME by Elizabeth Hoy (#526)
During the crossing to Ireland, Cathleen offered to take care of a small kitten. A friendly gesture, which had some far reaching consequences, leading her to some very strange — and exciting results!